BLACK TULIPS

Black Tulips

BRUCE EASON

TURNSTONE PRESS

Turnstone Press
607-100 Arthur Street
Winnipeg, Manitoba
Canada R3B 1H3

Turnstone Press gratefully acknowledges the assistance of the Canada Council and the Manitoba Arts Council in the publication of this book.

Cover illustration by Steve Gouthro, oil on panel.

This book was printed and bound in Canada by Kromar Printing Limited for Turnstone Press.

Canadian Cataloguing in Publication Data

Eason, Bruce, 1946-
Black tulips

ISBN 0-88801-160-1

I. Title.

PS8559.A865B52 1991 C813/.54 C91-097160-9
PR9199.3.E286B52 1991

For Mary Jane

The author is grateful to the Manitoba Arts Council for its financial support.

Some of these stories, or versions of them, first appeared in *Antigonish Review*, *Canadian Fiction Magazine*, *Fiddlehead*, *Grain*, *Prairie Fire*, and *Made in Manitoba: An Anthology of Short Fiction* (Turnstone Press). "The Appalachian Trail" is reprinted from *Open Windows: Canadian Short-Short Stories* by permission of Quarry Press.

Talking pessimistically is pleasant. If we were talking pessimistically it wasn't because we were convinced by what we were saying, but because black ideas, like black tulips, are the most beautiful.

—from "The Wedding Gown" by Réjean Ducharme. Translated by William Kinsley.

The night was windy and cold, he was warm under the sheets; the night was as big as a hill, he was a boy in bed.

—from "The Tree" by Dylan Thomas.

CONTENTS

THE APPALACHIAN TRAIL

Today she tells me it is her ambition to walk the Appalachian Trail, from Maine to Georgia. I ask how far it is. She says, "Some two thousand miles."

"No, no," I reply, "you must mean two hundred, not two thousand."

"I mean two thousand," she says, "more or less, two thousand miles long. I've done some reading too, about people who've completed the journey. It's amazing."

"Well, you've read the wrong stuff," I say. "You should've read about the ones who didn't make it. Those stories are more important. Why they gave up is probably why you shouldn't be going."

"I don't care about that, I'm going," she says with a determined look. "My mind is made up."

"Listen," I say, reaching for words to crush her dream. "Figure it out, figure out the time. How long will it take to walk two thousand miles?" I leap up to get a pen and paper. Her eyes follow me, like a cat that is ready to pounce.

"Here now," I say, pen working, setting numbers deep into the paper. "Let's say you walk, on average, twenty miles a day. That's twenty into two thousand, right? It goes one hundred times. And so, one hundred equals exactly one hundred years. It'll take you one hundred years!"

"Don't be stupid," she says. "One hundred *days*, not years!"

"Oh, yeah, okay, days," I mumble. I was never good at math. I feel as if someone has suddenly twisted an elastic band around my forehead. I crumple the paper, turn to her and say, "So if it's one hundred days, what is that? How many months?"

"A little over three." She calculates so fast that I agree without thinking. "Fine, but call it four months," I say, "because there's bound to be some delay: weather, shopping for supplies, maybe first aid treatments. You never know, you have to make allowances."

"All right, I make allowances, four months."

What have I done? It sounds as if all this nonsense is still in full swing. *Say more about the time.* "Okay," I say, "so where do we get the time to go? What about my job? What about my responsibilities, *your* responsibilities too? What about—"

"What about I send you a postcard when I finish the trip?" she says, leaving the room.

I sit there mouthing my pen. I hear her going down the basement steps. Pouting now, I think. Sulking. She knows she's wrong about this one.

"See my backpack?" she calls from below. God, she's really going to do it. "Next to mine," I say. "On the shelf beside the freezer."

I am angry with myself. She has had her way, won without even trying. "Take mine down too," I blurt out. "You can't expect to walk the Appalachian Trail all alone." I stare at my feet. "Sorry," I say to them both. "I'm bloody sorry about all of this."

THE BIG STEEL THING

The woman he liked, he took her to see this big steel thing. She said it was beautiful, that she had never seen anything quite like it before. *Mind-boggling* was the word she used. *Beautiful* and *mind-boggling.*

He disagreed. He said it looked *gross*, like some kind of *monstrosity*, like some kind of twisted shapeless thick-legged spider. "It don't do nothing for me," he said. "It don't make any sense to have it here neither. But I guess if that's what they want to do, we can't change their minds, can we? Whatever they want to do, they'll go ahead and do it, build these damn things and make us look at them. It all relates to the nature of man," he said. "It's the nature of man to screw things up."

He gave her a quick glance. He wanted to see if his words had impressed her. They must have, for she smiled and let him take her hand.

He had considered the phrase before saying it: *the nature of man*. But it still hadn't come out right; it didn't sound natural.

In the beginning, he found it necessary to pause, to think about what he was going to say. He hated doing that; it made him feel slow. But having said what he wanted, he believed all was okay; her smile, her eyes, and the way she held his hand, it felt good.

They walked around and admired the big steel thing some more as it glistened in the sun like a huge piece of ice. He started calling the big steel thing a *structure*. He used the word *structure* and she liked that. He didn't have to think about that word, it just popped into his head and came out of his mouth real easy, so he used the word again and forgot about *the nature of man*. She was tired of hearing him use *the nature of man* anyway and told him so: "I'm not sure," she said, "but it sounds sexist to me." She used the word *structure* too, but not as many times as he did.

"This here *structure*," he said. "It strikes me that the artist was thinking about the size more than anything else. He was trying hard to make the thing look as big as possible without having it fall over. He was only trying to impress on everyone how big he could make this steel thing look. Drawing attention to himself, that's all he was doing, trying to draw attention to himself. They all got these big ideas, you see? Egos. Artists with big egos, they like making big things, big *structures*."

After saying that, he felt pleased with himself, and they walked around a little more. Then, before she noticed, he spotted an old man relieving himself. He was urinating all over one of the steel thing's smooth silver legs. She saw the drunk too, saw him before he could let go of her hand to divert her attention or block her view.

"What's he doing there?" she asked, pulling his arm down. Then it dawned on her what the man was doing. "Oh!" she said. "Isn't that awful?" When the drunk heard her voice, he tried to zip up his fly and run at the same time. "Do you think that man knows what this steel thing is really for?" she asked.

"I don't think nobody knows what it's for," he answered seriously. "That's why it's here. They put it here to make you think, make you wonder, make all kinds of crazy things go through your head and mix you up. *Impressions*."

He liked that word too and decided to use it again. "*Impressions* on what life is all about," he said, and ran a hand through his thick hair. "I once read a story," he said, "about a man who tied himself up with a rope. He tied his whole body up so he couldn't move and somehow got onto a street corner where people could watch him struggle, but he couldn't get free. I can't remember who wrote that story and I don't know why it was written either, but I never forgot it. It made me think, think about life, you know? And that's what this thing is supposed to do, get you thinking about why it was made. Like that man and the rope, why was that thought up? Who knows?"

After he had said that, she looked at him without saying anything. Her dark eyes held him. They looked clear and beautiful. He put his arm around her and they walked under the big steel thing with the only sound being their steps and his hard breathing. Inside, with the steel legs all around them, he said they could easily be two little flies trapped in one of those fly-eating plants. She said that kind of thing was all right with her as long as something in nature was happy about it, as long as their dying had a purpose.

He didn't know why, but he felt confused about her saying that. Maybe it was because *she* now used the word *nature*, when he'd said *the nature of man*. He wasn't sure. He kissed her on the cheek anyway, and a feeling came over him, a good feeling about not having to think about anything, about not having to search for words to describe the big steel thing anymore.

Still standing inside, they held one another close as if afraid of the dark legs that rose over them. And then quickly she asked him about the suggestion he had made earlier: about their going somewhere for an ice cream cone.

Holding her the way he was, the thought of doing that,

eating something cold, made him shiver, but he agreed. When she stepped away from him, he followed her back onto the street. It was Sunday, the way he had always pictured Sundays: the church bells ringing in the distance, the street wet and black from a slow night rain, thousands of yellow leaves pressed flat on the ground. There was nothing wrong with it, the scene that is; he sensed it, understood it without having to draw on a word. But it was those other things, the ones they kept putting up, fitting in; the cramming troubled him. Not so much the big steel thing they had seen, but the other things, like the tall buildings and the new housing and the cars speeding by: the intrusions, the smothering, the buying, the getting. He was anxious to know how she felt about it, if she wanted to get away from it too. But he was afraid to ask her. He hadn't known her for very long.

They ate ice cream and walked. He began to tell her what he believed about the world, that the planet was probably nothing more than a speck of dust in God's eye. "Nothing more than that," he said. "And the longer it stays in there, the more it bugs Him. Some day, He's going to rub it, dig it out and squash us or flick us away. Flick us all into outer space or into the sun. What do you think of that?"

"That explains the water," she said.

"What?"

"The water. The salt water. His eyes. Don't you see? The tears in His eyes. They must be the oceans."

"Wow! You know, you might be right about that. I've never thought of it that way before." His voice grew higher. "Sure, sure, the oceans are His tears!" He pulled at his ear, smiling, thinking. He told her that the two of them should do something, see a professor somewhere, or see some "big shots" in the sciences to let them know about their new-found theory, "so that they might tell the world where the world really is."

They laughed. He liked her laughter. He wished he could hear it often, not just today. He thought of the worlds inside her eyes. He looked for them. He did not see them, but he wanted to bless her eyes and, to her surprise, he started kissing them. She broke free and said, "What are you doing?"

"I don't know," he answered.

"Then why don't we go home." It was a statement, not a question.

He agreed.

They walked along the sidewalk. The air felt much cooler now; the sun had disappeared. They came upon the big steel thing again. It seemed even more still, more lifeless, more grey than white against a darkening sky. They stopped, as though they ought to, to admire it one last time; he found it disturbing, tiring too. The way they had come full circle and how, once again, he found himself in search of a word.

ON DEATH AND SEX AND LAUGHING SQUIRRELS

Early spring: mild weather, a dog-crap smell. He sits in a wooden chair, sprawled. A coffee cup rests on the arm. Ugly snow. Everywhere he looks there is ugly snow and mud and pools of water and last year's leaves. He doesn't care for the winter up here, it has always been too long and too cold. Head back, eyes closed, he faces the sun. If only he didn't feel so sick the day would seem more bearable. Hey, people and dogs. BEWARE OF THE DOG: the sign tells him a lot about the owners, that they're as vicious as their animals. He's thinking dog because he hears one now, not far from where he sits. It barks loudly, frantic. Maybe the dog has treed a squirrel? Sure, that's what he's done.

Eyes closed, he pictures the squirrel. The squirrel bounces a pine cone off the dog's nose. The dog barks like crazy. The squirrel laughs.

"Hey, hey . . . that can't be," he says. "How can I see a laughing squirrel? What am I thinking?" He rubs his eyes, opens them, squints at the sky. It's Sunday. He was drunk on Saturday. Right now his stomach and head don't feel very good. He's sure that in such a condition, one should be more careful. It's possible to think and believe anything, become paranoid. It can start with a laughing squirrel, and end up with who knows what? Maybe taking another drink; and if that happens, he'll be drunk all over again. *Alcoholic?* He's not sure. And he won't quit long enough to find out how bad he really misses the stuff.

The logging trucks, the pothole makers, they're not hauling today. Sunday is a good day to take a walk, far enough to breathe a little deeper and get some of the stiffness out of his legs. He stands, stretches, then bends to tuck his pant cuffs inside his rubber boots. He sets off, and not far down the road he sees a boy and a dog, then soon realizes it isn't a boy after all, it's a woman. A woman, maybe his age, wearing a red and black checkered hunting jacket, blue jeans, bush boots, and a little blue hat. *Ah yes*, he believes the important brain cells will live. He plans a greeting: should I walk up to her? No, better to say hi from a distance. No, I'll smile first, then say hello, or better, start with a question. Maybe say, "Nice day, isn't it?" She'll have to answer that. He feels better already. The dog, though, he doesn't trust the dog. He's big and black and might be mean. The dog wags his tail. They are very close now, too close. He forgets to smile. He forgets his opening line. He forgets everything. He's too queasy, just a jumble of nerves all over again, too concerned about the dog, afraid she'll sic it onto him.

"Hey," she says.

"Yes?" he answers, flinching.

"Sorry, I didn't mean to frighten you."

"Oh, you didn't frighten me," he says, eyeing the animal and not her. The beast, head down, tongue out, wags its tail, comes to greet him, sniffing at his boots, then licking his hands. He rubs the dog's ears. The dog seems to like that.

"I think there's a body in the lake back there."

"Could be," he says, his mind unwilling to register words of death. He continues to scratch the dog but fears the worst, that what she's said is true. He doesn't want to see anything dead today, especially something once human. No, no, he thinks. No corpses today, thank you.

"Did you hear what I said?" she asks.

"Yes, I did," he replies. He leaves the dog alone and for the first time takes a real good look at the woman. Not what you'd call beautiful, but a certain something about her. She wears a lost look; for him that's easy to relate to.

Her outdoorsy clothes do nothing for her. Unattractive, except for the little blue hat: woollen, light blue with a lot of dime-sized snowflakes knitted in. Cute, he thinks. I bet her grandmother made it for her.

"Do you live near here?" she asks.

"Yes," he says. He turns and points. "Not far."

"Well, you should call the police then."

"I better have a look first." He has to be sure; he won't phone the police just on her say-so.

It takes about ten minutes to get to the train trestle. In that short time he finds out her name, the dog's name too, that she's separated with two kids, that she's come north to live with her brother and his wife. She hopes to find a job. She doesn't talk that much; he just asks a lot of questions. He tells her who he is and that he works in the mine. "I like the money—hate the job," he says. "I've been nursing a hangover all morning, but I'm feeling better now."

"I'm glad you're feeling better," she says. She looks as if she means it, and this pleases him.

At the train trestle, standing close, they look over the water. He's afraid to move, not because of the height but because he fears leaving her side; she might think he doesn't like her. As his eyes search for the body, pretty fingers touch his arm, tug on his jacket. He turns and sees a wet tongue sweep across soft lips. She points at the water. "There," she says, "over there. That's a body, isn't it?"

But dream-like he sees himself wearing a stupid grin, the one that shows up whenever he happens to be drunk, only this time he's not drunk. This time, like a lot of other times, he's fallen in love. His eyes follow her arm, her slender hand, the long slim finger which points out to a spot not far from where they're standing, to a place where a dark object floats with melting ice. He's never seen a drowned person before, and although he takes the woman's hand, he's not afraid, but self-assured, keen on knowing her better. He's curious too—finds it strange how the dead float: face down, arms reaching, reaching towards the bottom, as if the body's trying to reach out to embrace someone or catch a running child. The legs are bent and wide apart like a toy cowboy moulded to fit a plastic horse.

"Look at the long hair," she whispers to him. But instead he watches her hair: so long, so straight, so black, so lovely.

"Do you think it's a woman?"

"Yes, I think you're right," he says, "a woman." He's relieved they can't see the face. What a nightmare it would be if they could. Outdoor deaths are usually ugly ones, disturbing. You can't prepare for them. They happen suddenly, in a flash, right in front of you. Or you might come across one, like this. When his grandfather died, everyone was ready, prepared. They expected it. In fact, all the family was in a rush to get to the funeral parlour, if only to see who might be there. The only disturbance was when his little brother wanted to know how they got all the blood out of him.

"We can't do anything here," he says to her. "We might as well go back and phone the police."

They leave hand in hand. The dog runs to greet them.

"I hardly know you," she says. "Why are we holding hands?"

"It's the north," he says. "You're not used to it, are you? We're friendly up here, always friendly."

She smiles. She knows it's a line. He knows she knows it's a line. He's always saying stupid things like that to women, sometimes believing his own stuff. He doesn't even know if they like what he tells them, or why it pleases him to say it.

They reach the house, the shack; he bought it cheap. There's no running water. But there is electricity. Going in, she tells the dog to stay; the animal settles itself down on the broken step, the only step.

"Have you been in this place *long*?" she asks, as if he were doing time.

"About three years," he replies. "I know it's not much of a place, but it's all I need. It's warm and dry. Well, not so warm but dry. Except in the spring, like now, the roof leaks." He points to the water dripping in the porch, a puddle on the floor. "I don't cook much. I eat in town. Shower at work. Sometimes I even go in for a shower on my days off. Would you like a drink?"

Her eyes are wide and blue and wet as if the air has hurt them. "Do you have any beer?"

"Well, let's see," he says. He opens the fridge. "No. Rye. All we've got is ice-cold rye whisky. Some pig drank all the beer last night. I saw him in the mirror this morning. He looked terrible!"

"You're crazy," she says.

All the glasses are dirty. He takes out the bottle, opens the cupboard and finds two coffee cups. "I don't want to be around to watch them pull her out, do you?" He fills the cups half full of whisky. "Sure glad we couldn't see her face," he says, handing her the best-looking mug.

"Seeing her face. That would be awful," she says and makes herself shiver. "Do you have any mix?"

"Water. Is that okay?"

"Fine."

He goes to a white bucket and lifts a dipper out.

"Water's all I use too," he says. "There's no ice but I can break a piece off the roof—"

"No, this is fine. Are you going to call the police now?"

"Let's have our drinks first."

He doesn't want to phone right away. He's never been in trouble with the law—well, not much anyway—but to him, people in uniform act funny, make you nervous. They talk as though they're afraid of something, as though you might be out to get the better of them. Maybe it's image. They climb all over you to protect their image.

They sit on an old couch. He can feel his blood warming. He feels better, happy, glad to be alive, a drink in his hand, a woman beside him. *Ah yes, love makes everything better. Makes the world go around. Something like that.*

He clicks his cup against hers. "Here's how," he says. "Here's how I lost the farm." He gulps his drink, takes all of it. One swig and *liquid fire!* For a second, he doesn't think it's going to stay down. She sips at hers and makes a face. He gets the water bucket and whisky bottle and quickly returns. He puts the bucket at their feet. He pours another drink. She hasn't finished her first, but says nothing about him adding more. He puts his arm around her. They place their drinks on a little table, an empty apple box. They begin to kiss: long, wet, and warm. He slips her jacket off. He opens her blouse. She wears no bra. Her breasts are small, the nipples taut. They seem to eye him. He doesn't hesitate to mouth them. Although death is nearby, life beckons. They undo and pull off clothes and toss them to the floor. Fear and the urge to enter grip his brain, tighten. While their limbs are roped together, he feels crazed, drugged: the words, the words that aren't words, they come out and echo off the walls like some ungodly chant. Lips kiss and hiss and miss. Suck air. They spit and blow out groans and moans. A line without meaning slips in: *Am I a beetle or a bee?* And then, he hears himself speak without knowing why he says what he says. Maybe it's because she hasn't bothered to take it off and he's afraid she might.

"Please, leave the little blue hat on," he blurts out, his voice strangely high, begging.

"What?"

"Your little blue hat, don't take it off."

"You're perverted?" she asks, smiling shyly.

"Yes," he answers without shame. "I think I am."

The little blue hat remains. It's wonderful, he thinks, how she knows him, how she understands his silliness, his needs.

Death. The shadows are behind him now. The dog barks. The squirrel laughs. Seeing the squirrel, he thinks, *bless the squirrel.* He's ready. He feels hard for her. He hopes to be for the longest time: pumping joy, pumping on and on.

Quickly, it's over, he's out. Nothing left to do but hold her now. Hold her, once, twice, roll away and stare at the ceiling. He listens to the water drip in the porch. She straightens her hat. She tells him he's the best she's ever had. He doesn't answer. He knows it's a line. She knows that he knows it's a line. He'll phone the police now. Standing, pulling on his pants, he begins to think that some day this whole damn shack will become one big soggy hunk of cardboard and fold right in on top of him.

MILE 84

Beside a lake and a half day's journey past a yellow sign where the wind blew songs between the eaves of a large cabin a man abandoned a woman and a child and a large long-legged beast who waited for a chance to be gone too. The woman did not blame the beast for wanting to go. Even when the man was there, she had known aloneness and that animals felt it too. Sometimes she thought seclusion lived outside herself and took pleasure in the way it could subdue her mind, making her thoughts hurt and difficult to focus. Sometimes the stillness in the big room was accompanied by ghost-like illusions: flat white clouds that descended from the axe-hewed rafters and swirled and wrapped her young body into a tight cocoon that caused pains up and down her arms and in her stomach and legs. Sometimes the emptiness would become so unbearable that the woman would place a hand upon her breast or flat against her forehead and fear fainting. The idea of falling unconscious in front of the child was frightening, so she would hurry off to bed, close her wet blue eyes, and wait for the moment to pass. Often this took a long time.

* * *

"How do I know they're game wardens?" the trapper mumbled to himself. "How do I know you're really game wardens?" he shouted from the door. "How do I know you ain't come here to steal things, bust up my place?"

"Well, look at our jackets then," one of them called. "Can't you tell by our jackets?" He pointed to a cloth patch on his shoulder. "See, GAME WARDEN marked here." He tapped the yellow lettering with his finger.

"That don't mean nothing to me," the trapper said. "You can have any kind of crest sewed onto a jacket. I can't be sure who you guys really are."

"Well, let us come closer to show our ID's—"

"No sir! You stay right there. Or, better yet, get off my trapline. I've got a rifle here."

The wardens eyed each other, nodded. They weren't going to take any chances. They stepped backward and disappeared into the woods.

The trapper figured they must have gotten off the train at mile 84, near the yellowed sign; the same place he got off whenever he came from town. But he hadn't been to town lately. He hadn't been to town for a long time. *What brought them here anyway?* Maybe they wanted to find out why he was cutting a line. Why a man cuts a trail just for himself. *It's not so wide. I'm sure they can't see it from the air.*

"How are you today, sir?" one of the wardens had asked him, sounding real friendly, as if he was actually interested in how the trapper was doing. *I know it was no social call. I know that! By God, they better be gone. They better be gone or I'll be shooting.* "You hear? I'll shoot!" He lifted the rifle up and swung it around. The end of the barrel hit the stove-pipe. The pipes came apart and fell with a loud clang. Soot and smoke billowed up and blackened the cabin air. "Bloody hell! Where's the door? The latch!" He found the latch; he grabbed hold of it and flicked it up and swung the door wide open; he stumbled into the light. As he breathed in, the air felt good, cold. It felt like crushed ice melting over his dry lungs. There were snowshoes on a nail. He took one down and shovelled up a big scoop of snow. He ran back inside and threw the snow inside the stove. The fire sizzled out. Then, making certain, he went out to see if the wardens had really gone; eyeing and following their tracks, he stopped and listened every so often until he felt satisfied that they weren't anywhere near his place. The ore trains went by three times a day and he figured they'd be catching the next one out soon.

* * *

The beast waited and heard the child outside. The mother watched from the window as the child played near the lake. The lake was deep but hard with ice. The mother was thinking that in the wintertime, dressed so warm, you can fall against anything and not be hurt. She thought about eating too. She thought about baking something sweet. She had had a daydream about peaches. How the juice squirted and dripped on her chin. How the man's tongue licked her chin and how they behaved when the peach was finished.

* * *

It was a dirty struggle to get the pipes up again. He rebuilt the fire and left the door open to air the cabin out. He didn't try to clean the soot off the floor. The floor was made of rough boards; it didn't matter to him that it was dirty.

* * *

The cabin air was warm. The walls were sweating. The woman wondered why she would follow a man to such a remote place as this. For that matter, why would any woman want to follow any man anywhere at all? What had love to do with it? Was it my weakness? she thought. Am I weak to want a man? No. But to go so far away? Yes. It was dumb to think I could be happy here.

* * *

Not hearing a voice, the animal moved away from the fire. He sat beside the door and waited. The child opened the door. The animal saw its chance and flew out like a bat.

"Oh Mother!" the child cried. "He's out! I'm sure he's gone for good."

"Let him go," she ordered, gripping a bowl more tightly although it wasn't turning or falling.

* * *

In the night, the fire crackled its familiar sleepy heat. He ate his supper and lit the lamp, chewed tobacco and stared at the lamp's yellow flame. He looked from the lamp to the set of aviation books on the table. They were in a neat stack ten high. Each book had a hard brown cover. Soot dotted the top one and he reached over and brushed it off. The books were a first edition, 1921. Although he did not know how to read and did not know numbers very well, he liked the books. He liked to thumb through the pages and study the fine three-dimensional drawings, the fine print on the thin yellow pages. When tired, he would place them all in a neat pile again. He had bought the books at a sale in town: ten hard-covered books, stacked beside a number of pocket books. Cost: fifty cents each.

The wind had picked up. He lay on the bed with the lamp out. Pulling up a down-filled sleeping bag, he thought he heard someone talking, but then decided it must be nothing more than some tree limbs rubbing together or the fire burning. Eyes closed, he dreamed the same dream: the house, the children in their beds. The wife? He didn't know where the wife was. There was heat and smoke and then everything became flame. *The children!* The fire was everywhere. The flames leaped wave-like and danced all over the stairs, the walls, the ceiling. There was no chance to break through or come around the flames and the children were calling. Everything was burning, his clothes too. He saw himself on the ground, on the lawn, rolling over and over. "No! No!" he yelled, sitting up awake, sweating, panting like a runner. "Here! Here! Here!" he yelled in the night. *A dream! Out of my head! Damn you dream!* He threw his hands over his face and sobbed long sobs. When his heart stopped racing, he eyed the stove, watched it glowing. The stove's belly looked like some gigantic orange-red eye. There's devils in there, he thought, pulling on his boots, and in his long-johns he opened the door and stepped outside. Shivering in the winter cold, he unbuttoned his fly, reached down and yellowed the snow. There was a wolf. It howled. The animal was near the lake where the trapper netted fish. He howled at the howl, then all was silent again. The wind died down and the world was empty and senseless, as senseless as a faceless watch in a dark cold pocket. He hurried in, stood by the stove and rubbed his hands together. The dream was gone, forgotten. He took the lid off the stove and banked it with new wood, then got into bed and told himself that all was well, that it was just like it was before, except that those game wardens' tracks were all over the place. But as soon as it snows, he thought, the tracks will be gone, then everything will be back to normal, the way it was before they came, the way he wanted it to be: with the fish heads, the traps, the furs, the skinning and the stretching and the smell of it and the red drops sunk in the pure white snow and the gut feed for the ravens and the whiskeyjacks. Although he didn't like the whiskeyjacks. They were always whistling what sounded like "*Your* tears! *Your* tears! *Your tears!*" And when the trapping fell off, he was never lost for anything to do, for there was always that seemingly endless trail to blaze.

* * *

In a windless night where the sharp air cleansed the senses, sterilized the eyes, there was a quarry, a rabbit in the snow. The animal saw it and gave chase, but the chase was cut short, for a great horned owl swooped down and caught the rabbit by the neck and lifted it high. And with the rabbit screaming, the beast with saliva dripping like hot wax could only snap at the moon.

* * *

"Where do you think he'll go?" asked the child.

"Where most of them go," said the mother. She looked up from the bowl and gazed at a thick fur coat that hung from a hook on the door. "He's going where he feels more alive."

"In the night?" said the child.

* * *

There was another scent and more running and running and everything beat harder and harder and faster and faster through the body and through the head, especially in front of the ears, just above the brow, where the new images liked to dance. And what was jelled melted warm, then hot, to flow hot, to flow like a river in spring as the woods whipped past the eye.

* * *

"Do you think he'll come back?"

"I doubt it," said the mother. "He hurts. His need is greater than ours."

* * *

In the night, the trail showed one like himself, one that had been running too, running out long and hard. They stopped short. They eyed each other in the stillness and listened and watched with the night holding, hanging cold and weighted. He shifted, sniffed, caught her scent and strained for more, then slithered towards her, brushing her side. Playfully, before darting away, she nipped him on the neck; he yelped and jumped in behind her.

* * *

"I'm not missing him," said the child. "I'm not missing anyone—anymore."

"Come here and help me make biscuits," said the mother. "When you smell the biscuits baking in the oven your tummy will feel hungry and rumble."

Then came a howling that sent a shiver like a long thin sliver of ice straight up and down the spine. "Do you think it's him?"

"Of course it is; he knows we're here and hearing him." She removed her apron. She took a wet cloth and wiped the flour from the board she had rolled the dough on.

"When will the biscuits be ready?"

"When you are ready for bed." She smiled at the clean little face; the skin looked so new. In the child's corner, they spoke in whispers, feeling close, but close to the edge of night too, as though the night might come in at any time if it wanted.

"If he comes back, will you let him in?"

"I'm afraid that I will," said the mother.

"Do you love him?"

"Love him?"

"Why would he run away?"

She brushed the child's hair across the forehead, bent low and kissed the tiny red mouth. In her room she lay down and felt the night all around her. She imagined what was in the woods beside her, what was awake running free and alive, wild, unthinking. She wanted to grab the dark, to hold onto the night, to pull the darkness inside herself. She wanted to stop the dark from leaving, from dissolving. She could hide in the dark, in the pain. She would allow the pain to come through before the light came in to show the cabin and to move her in a way she did not want to move.

* * *

In the morning the trapper's cabin was crackling cold. The plastic on the little window was clear enough that he could see the sun shining. The stove still held a few hot coals. He put some more wood on, stoked it up and got the fire going again. Steamed fish and boiled rice filled him for breakfast. The trapper felt strong and, as usual, lonely too. For no matter what the chore, at some level aloneness was always with him. When he felt it really near, he called it "dead-time." It was like suddenly dropping into a deep hole. It didn't matter what the season was either, nor the hour. When dead-time took over, it took pleasure at gnawing at the insides. And then there would come that last-man-on-earth business. Sometimes it would come on him in the woods and he would lean against a tree to moan and let the tears flow. After crying, everything would be all right for a time. Having it, feeling it, was like some strange cycle he had to go through. But aloneness could come on him at any moment, like a fit.

This morning, he took his axe and moved a little fir tree away from where the trail started. Then he walked up to where he had left off and blazed some more, cutting trees for no one but himself and whatever might want to hide under them. He liked to see the line grow longer and longer, long and deep through the bush, way out past the railroad tracks, far west, past the yellow sign, the sign that had black letters and black numbers showing: Mile 84.

Young saplings fell as fast as if he were slicing cane. His body pumped hot in the cold air and steamed while he swung his axe. It had been some time since he had looked up. Only after he had blazed the trail to a treeless spot did he straighten to see what he had done and where he stood. He was surprised to see that he had cut his way to a small lake, and was even more surprised when he spotted a cabin on the other side. *A log cabin. A large one.* He watched a stream of white smoke curl from a stone chimney. He thought that he had time to walk across the frozen lake and home again before dark; that is, if he wanted to, but he did not want to. He was afraid to move. The thought of walking in that direction stiffened him. The more he looked at the cabin, the more he imagined someone there. The very idea of greeting another, introducing himself, shaking hands, speaking; it was all so impossible, so unfamiliar, unlike confronting game wardens. Here so long, what could he hope to say? More sweat. Not a working sweat, but a thought-filled fearful sweat. When he turned to leave, the cold dug deeper, clawed, hurt like sharp fingernails.

The next morning, before breakfast, he put on a parka and went out to check the traps. There was a red fox in one. He was taking it out when they grabbed him. They took him by the arms and put their own steel traps around his wrists. They led him to the railroad track. He was feeling different now, very tired and weak, too weak to fight with anyone. He wanted to say something, but the train whistle blared and he forgot what it was he wanted to say. The engine stopped right at the yellow sign: Mile 84. The three of them climbed black steel stairs and entered a green passenger car. They sat him near a window. The ore train pulled away. He looked through the window and watched as the train passed the familiar trails, the frozen lakes, the spot where the line was cut. He thought about the large cabin, the one he had seen across a lake. For sure, he would never know anything about the place now. The train moved faster and faster. One of the men offered him a mint. "What are they?" the trapper asked as he reached for one. "Candies," said the Mountie. "Bet you haven't had one for a long time."

"Bet you're right," said the trapper. He fingered one out of the bag and popped it straight into his mouth.

* * *

The animal returned. There was blood on its back. The woman held the door while the creature limped in. The child cried for him. The mother stood the animal in a tub filled with warm water and began to wash where she thought the wounds might be.

"What do you think happened?"

"He was fighting—wanting a bitch," the mother said. Her voice was low. She gazed at the water turning red.

"You fought for a bitch?" The child held the animal's large head in both hands and stared long and fierce into its sad dark eyes. "Did you win?"

"There's worlds, different worlds," the mother said, not saying anything more but knowing that people and other living things were in these worlds and did not know why. Not many would get out either. But a few might act, feel their blood and do what their blood told them to do. Like the beast, when his hot blood made him run wild in the woods in a search.

She drew away to let the animal step from the tub; he shook himself and sprayed the child, who laughed. They watched the animal go to the fire where he walked twice in a circle, then lay down. Then they heard the train. The floor quivered. The animal's ears lifted and listened. The woman and the child looked at each other and listened too. The beast licked himself and then was levelled by the warmth of the fire: heavy head down, legs and body flatly sprawled, eyelids lowered. Soon he was sleeping. The woman sensed a newness about the beast and within herself too. The beast had come back in pain, hurt but satisfied, renewed. Now, if the man returned, she was sure: she and the child would leave. The thought of leaving the place held firm and pleased her. She felt new strength. And the beast, if the beast wanted to go, she would let him go anytime. There was no reason to stop anything from happening now, no reason to stop herself from trying, from being brave and daring. She took the child's hand. She made herself a promise to open the door each day, to breathe the air and watch for hints of spring; the world and night could long for themselves. Some early morning, she'd slip away as the beast had done. On the other side of the lake, she'd go and find the steel rails, so she and the child could wait and listen and wave and watch for the train to pull to a halt. And, because there are no conductors on ore trains, "All aboard," she'd say to the little one, "all aboard. . . ."

ELROY AND THE FOLKS UPSTAIRS

Elroy woke with a start. They were at it again. He heard furniture moving. A thud. Another thud. *Was that her head? Was he banging her head on the floor?*

He heard words. Swear words. They came loud and clear, as if the two of them were fighting right inside Elroy's bedroom and not upstairs.

"Bastard!" she yelled. "I wish you were dead, you prick!" *Slaps.* Elroy pictured a hard flat hand smacking. *Smacking what? Smacking her face? Her arm? Where is he hitting her?* Sobs turned into child-like whimpering.

"Think you, think you know it all—you slut! A guy can't have a couple of beers? What do you expect me to do? Sit around this fuckin' hole and suck my thumb?"

"I don't care what you do," she yelled. "Just leave me alone, leave me alone or get out! Get out! I hate you!"

"Don't tell me to get out of my own place, you bitch!"

Elroy turned on the light and put on his eyeglasses. The clock showed near 2:00 a.m. He tossed the covers off, got out of bed and paced the room. I ought to go up there, he thought. I ought to go up there and bang on the door, tell them I can't sleep, tell them politely to tone it down.

Feet raced across the bedroom ceiling, a woman's run. "No! No! No!" she screamed. "Don't do that!" There was a loud clunk—something had fallen—then silence. The stillness made Elroy's stomach tighten. *What's he doing to her now? Is he trying to kill her? Is he choking her? I have to do something. I can't just hole up here and pretend nothing is happening.*

They had moved in two weeks ago. Already this was their second fight and it sounded a lot worse than their first. The last time, there was no banging around, only words. This time, someone was really getting it. Elroy wasn't sure what she looked like. But he thought he had seen her partner one day last week, coming out of the parking lot: a big man, a man with a bushy moustache and eyes that slanted hard and mean when he saw Elroy looking at him, so that Elroy shied, looked the other way.

Elroy pulled on his red and white striped dressing-gown, slipped into his bedroom slippers. He couldn't believe how bad his hands were shaking. Fear channelled through him. He was shivering. He felt as if his blood had chilled and was seeping into corners it had never known before.

Elroy opened the door and stepped out into the hall. He hurried down the hallway and opened the fire door, ran upstairs, opened the fire door on that landing too, took a few steps and faced the apartment. He listened. He heard nothing. Knocked. Hesitated. Knocked again. Knocked a little louder this time. Heard someone mumble. Heard footsteps. "What do you want?" an old woman's voice hissed.

"Damn," Elroy whispered. In all his fear and trembling, he had knocked on the wrong door.

Elroy didn't say a word. He sneaked down to the right apartment where, inside, a woman was crying. He took a deep breath, raised his fist and knocked fast twice. The door unlocked, swung open. It was him, the same guy he had seen in the parking lot. He was shirtless. He looked like a man who worked out, pumped iron. There was a tattoo on his right shoulder: a snake with an arrow running through its skin, and three little dark heart shapes, symbolizing blood dripping from the arrow's tip.

"What's bothering you?" the fellow said, eyes narrowing, hairy chest expanding.

"Hi, I live downstairs," Elroy said and swallowed hard. "Heard you . . . heard someone make a noise up here. I was wondering if everything was all right. It sounded as if someone was having trouble, as if someone was being—"

"Listen fart face, you got trouble sleeping, you stuff something in your big fat ears, see?" When he spoke, the fellow's bushy moustache rose up and down like a whisk. He stuck a big finger on Elroy's narrow chest. "Anytime me and my woman have a disagreement, that's our business, see? I want you to understand that—understand it *real* good, because if you don't get what I mean, then you might be the one who has the trouble, get it?" He poked Elroy hard then, hard enough for Elroy to lose his balance, and he had to take a quick step backwards to regain it.

"No need to get testy," Elroy started to say. "I . . . I just wanted to be sure—" But the door slammed so hard that a big gust of wind, which smelled of stale beer, caught Elroy straight in the face.

Elroy took his time going downstairs. He wasn't shaking anymore. In fact, he was cursing the whole situation. It was useless to phone the caretakers, he had done that once before. All he got was a "Sorry" from an answering machine, "we're not in right now, but if you leave your name . . ." The caretakers were lucky enough, or rather, smart enough, to get themselves out of the building every Friday night, staying away for the whole weekend, every weekend.

No sooner had Elroy gotten into bed than there was a terrible crash; he figured something like a plate or a lamp had hit the hardwood floor and shattered. Then he heard slaps again and more whimpering. Then came that God-awful stomach-churning silence that sought out the mind's worst fears and played around with them.

"That's it! That's it!" Elroy said. "I won't have it. I pay my rent. I'm not listening to this all night. I'm calling the police."

There must have been a car in the area, because once the silence broke there were only a few more thumps and a couple more "fuck you's" and then Elroy knew the police had arrived. He heard knocking, and while they were knocking he thought about the look on the man's face as he came to open the door and then saw two officers standing there instead of Elroy.

There were words. Elroy couldn't make out too much this time, but he did hear the woman say, "No, no, I'm okay." Then it sounded as if the cops were walking around the apartment. He heard a man say, "It's not mine." Doors or drawers were being opened and slammed closed. He heard a toilet flush, then everything went quiet again. For a time, Elroy lay there watching the bedroom ceiling. At last he turned the light off and tried to fall asleep. Eventually he did. It was sunrise when he awoke to the sound of someone rapping on his door.

"What is it?" Elroy asked, opening the door enough to peek out. A woman was standing there in an ugly green dressing-gown that reached all the way down to a pair of fluffy blue slippers. She was a short, stocky woman with a puffy face and orange hair and black circles around sleepy eyes. A bloodless cut looked painful at the corner of her mouth. She took a quick drag on the cigarette she was holding and said, "You came upstairs last night, didn't you? It was you who phoned the fuckin' cops on us, wasn't it? Well, I just thought you might want to know that thanks to you and your call, they found Lenny's gun and then this bag of dope he was keeping for a friend. *Sonofabitch*. They took him to the station." She stopped for a second, ran a hand through her orange hair, coughed and took another drag on the cigarette. "Now he might go back to jail," she said. "All because you phoned the fuckin' cops. None of this wouldn't have happened if you hadn't had phoned the fuckin' cops. *Sonofabitch.* I don't know what Lenny might do. I mean like, he's unpredictable. Like when he gets pissed off, see? Like the way he is with you right now, pissed off. And what does Lenny tell me before he leaves? Lenny says, 'I'll get that little fucker, you wait and see if I don't.' That's what Lenny says—meaning you. Shit, sometimes people make noises, that happens. You shouldn't have done anything. Now you gotta face the consequences. Fuck, you know, some people are so fuckin' stupid, it makes a person want to scream. Why the fuck did you have to go and call the fuckin' cops anyway?"

She didn't wait for Elroy to reply. She dropped her smoke on the floor, in front of the door, and stepped on the butt, twisted it back and forth with her right slippered foot. Amazing, Elroy thought, right in the hallway, right on the hardwood floor. She gave Elroy a fierce look, as if daring him to say something about anything, then she pulled the long green robe in tight against her chest and marched off down the hall.

Elroy closed the door. With hands inside the pockets of his robe, he turned and leaned against the door and stared into the living room, stared at the furniture and over at the furthest wall, where a large picture hung: a cheap and faded-looking print that showed a field, and a mountain, and a bit of blue-white sky. Elroy shook his head. A strange kind of calm came over him. He knew what he had to do. He had little time to waste. But he was going to have a shower first, get dressed, make himself a good breakfast, a good hearty breakfast, before packing.

In the grave—nothing but slush and mud and wet snow—who'll bother about the likes of you?

Fyodor Dostoevsky, *Notes from Underground*

MY FIRST FUNERAL EVER

Three weeks ago, my grandpa died. It was my first funeral ever, the first time I ever saw anyone dead before, I mean, in real life—no TV stuff. So it's like I'm all shook up about going to see him, and I'm wondering all kinds of crazy things, like am I going to faint or get sick or do something weird right in front of everybody? Maybe throw up in the coffin, something real nuts-o like that. Anyway, I get in there and I think everyone is watching me, waiting for my reaction, like they're going to see me cry or break down or something. And then, I see him, my grandfather. He's flat out in the coffin with his arms folded, looking real peaceful like, as if he's content as hell about being where he is. And I don't feel nothing bad about it neither. I don't even feel sick or faint or nothing, just maybe a little tired like maybe I ought to go and sit next to my grandmother, not because I want to sit next to her, but for some reason that's the only chair left. So that's what I do. I go over to my grandmother. I sit down beside her and say, "Hello, Grandma. . . ." And she looks at me as if she's seeing me for the first time in her life. And then, she lets out this God-awful sound and I almost fall off my seat. It was like a wailing I had never heard before. It started real low, way down near the floor somewheres, and then it got running up higher and higher until it seemed to reach and finish off somewhere near the lights up on the ceiling. She scared the living hell out of me. Right then and there, I thought we'd be having another funeral. I tried to make a move to get away but, just as I do that, here if she doesn't go and reach over for me and gives me this God-awful bear hug and starts shaking and sobbing all over my hands and neck and face and finally ends up with her head on my shoulder. That's what got me feeling sick to my stomach, right then with her hangin' and bawlin' all over me. I couldn't get away and I couldn't breathe neither. I got real scared and I thought I was going to faint or throw up or kick her in the shins, or do something mean, or scream myself. I didn't like the way she was carrying on. You see, I knew how she didn't like that old man. I know she never loved him none. She was just putting on a big show for everyone to see. I couldn't get out of that place fast enough. And right now, I'm in a bind. We're supposed to go and visit her this Sunday coming; and as sure as angels sing, I won't be able to look Grandma in the eye.

THE ANTITOXIN

1

We're like termites, the heat drives us out, thinks Don Paul, stopping, being careful where he steps. There are squared patches of ground and he doesn't like to crush the grass. Not long ago, a farmer grew a crop here, and today it's a field of blacktop. Don Paul thinks progress has a way of smoothing things out, making life appear dull and flat like the hot pavement.

Don Paul has a letter to mail, a letter for a friend who never writes. He opens the mailbox and peeks inside. The box is almost full of letters. He wonders if it's possible to reach in and take one. Don Paul won't try, but pretends he has one. He makes believe it is a letter addressed to him, from his first love. She says she has left her husband and children and all she thinks about is Don Paul. She remembers their good times. She'll do anything to bring them back again. She'll do anything to please him. "Anything you desire," she writes. "I'm yours alone." Then her words become strained; she asks for money. The poor girl needs money for food and rent. Without enough money, she's afraid of becoming a whore, doing naughty things to dirty old men, just to make a life. "It's up to you," she says. Don Paul is the one to decide what will become of her. What can he do? She doesn't know how it is with him, how he hates responsibility, how he can't make decisions. "I don't even know her anymore. I don't even know myself." Don Paul steps quickly; he is no longer amused by his letter game. "Why do I make up such foolish games? Is life so dull?"

Don Paul pretends to crumple the letter. He opens his hands as if allowing the letter to fall. Inside the supermarket, Don Paul suddenly realizes what he's done: to discard the letter *is* a decision. Doing nothing can change a person's life. *Breathing is enough to cause trouble.*

He reaches for a shopping cart. He pulls on one but gets three. He struggles to unlock them. When one comes loose, Don Paul takes hold of it and pushes it down the aisle. He's here, but not hungry. He lies to the few people he does know. He says he's on a diet. He doesn't want anyone to know the truth: he's lost all taste for food.

He reaches for a box of cereal. Sometimes he closes his eyes. Fresh fruit and boxes aren't too hard to handle, but the meat is a horror. Don Paul hasn't touched meat for weeks.

He hurries with his cart: past the chicken gizzards, past the pigs' feet, past the smoked fish. He happens to glance at the baby beef liver soaking in its own blood. My God, he thinks, what we won't cut and choose from life, for life. And beef tongue? Who decides how much to charge for beef tongue?

Don Paul turns away. Across from him, he sees a woman with a baby boy. The child is sitting in the shopping cart with his legs dangling outside the basket. He kicks out at her. He jerks and twists and strains to grab what is on the shelves. Everything is too far away from him; he looks at her and yells baby profanities. She doesn't respond. She's too concerned with the price of rice. Don Paul wants to give him something, anything to shut him up. But he's afraid the mother might start to scream. He decides not to interfere. No, better to move along, stay in line. After all, he thinks, that's what it's all about, isn't it? Keeping ourselves in line?

At the checkout, Don Paul becomes conscious of the supermarket music which never works for him. It only seems to add more weight to what he breathes. His mind wonders, analyzes. He doesn't want to call it air: call it "stuff" or "mix." Real air died a long time ago. Nature sneaks up that way. *She* says, "I've changed. You don't recognize me, do you, all of this stuff and mix they've spilt all over me? But I'll get them back, you'll see." Don Paul knows it's true. He can feel it coming. Nature. She'll surprise everyone with her revenge.

He places his bananas and apples and box of cereal on top of the counter. The clerk says hello without feeling. The woman weighs and rings up the price of the fruit, then zips the cereal box across a little glass window. A computer voice says how much it is. Don Paul wonders why they don't get the machine to greet you. Like the clerk, it could say "hello" the same way every time. His change is dropped into a little grey bowl. *We don't touch fingers anymore.* He has no love for these machines. They're cold, indifferent, and they rush him.

What keeps Don Paul alive is placed into a plastic bag. He lifts it by the handles and walks out through the automatic doors. Outside, he meets the jogger. The guy who runs rain or shine. Don Paul usually nods. But this time, with the jogger near, Don Paul takes a deep breath and shouts: "You can't cheat death!" The jogger's eyes bulge. They look as big as tennis balls. Don Paul smiles. He feels good about knowing what the jogger fears. Don Paul opens the shopping bag and peeks inside. His heart is beating faster. His hands tremble. This has happened before: saying something, doing something, something new, something out of the ordinary, and then his body begins to shake, and his stomach begins to feel hungry, the way it's feeling now. *Youthful.*

* * *

In his room, at the window, eating a banana. A storm approaches: thick clouds form, billowing up and rolling together; fire-white forks of lightning and loud thunderclaps escape the black soup clouds. Don Paul thinks how fine it is to have the silence end. He understands that the world beckons him, but he refuses her invitation. His father's death has made it too easy. Because Don Paul invested what he could wisely, there's money for a room, like this one, and food, if he wants food. But the inheritance did not come with a purpose, only the means to exist, only a room with a window, only a place to open tins. That is his guarantee. It comes with a search for something he cannot name: God? Love? Sex? Companionship? Hope? Joy? Work? *No, not work.* But the possibilities are endless. They fall like rain. Ah yes, the rain . . . the first drops come: large, wetting the pavement black, hitting like bombs—that is, if one can imagine being a high-flying pilot. Crack! More thunder. Another flash of lightning. It begins to pour. The slowpokes are caught. They run. They panic. "Quick, get inside or you'll get wet!" They are confused. They are like the jogger, shocked by new directions.

If I had a purpose, thinks Don Paul, something straight, conventional, acceptable, enjoyable, *purposeful.* What would it mean and what would it be? Perhaps to build something. Something lasting. Solid, like a house. Would the project be worthwhile? Would it give me satisfaction? Or would it be only so much energy expelled, wasted? I must ask these questions; even if there are no answers, I must ask them anyway. Right now, all the hope is in the asking.

He eats banana number two. He chews it slowly. His stomach groans. He burps. His aloneness is evident to him as he stands in front of the window. He is doing what all lonely people do. They look out a window. They watch.

He eats. But he is not full, nor empty. His stomach, like his life, seems to sit there waiting for something good to happen to it.

He hears the mouse. The mouse comes out of its hole, into the bigger hole, the room. Oh mouse, Don Paul thinks, you are like me, your nest is bare. You survive on crumbs. With God and love gone, do you think about everything and believe nothing? Good for you if you do. You are more than a mouse to me. Your colour is the world. You reflect the in-between, the grey, the invisible signs, the only ones that count, the only ones that move. So why is the jogger running? He runs hard to become what? To feel fit? To buy another car? To build a bigger home? To appease the wife? To be in good shape for Doctor Death? Oh, so afraid to think about that question, aren't you? Maybe that is the best reason for your running—to stop yourself from thinking about everything in general, as everything in general is what makes your ulcer bleed. See him inside the house, breathing hard, soaked to the skin, running shoes squeaky wet, the wife yelling that the floors have just been cleaned. She tosses him a towel. He's treated like a dog. She'll feed him when his feet are dry. Give yourself a good shake, *woolly man.*

"Oh, Daddy!" his children cry. "Oh, Daddy. You look so terrible. So wet!"

"Yes, I'm wet, wet clean through, feeling great though. It's wonderful to run in the rain." So, the silly man gets sick. He's sick for a week, maybe two. His wife, in the middle of company, forces a smile, but secretly wishes him dead. It has all been too long, much too long, one long miserable sacrifice for the sake of the children. It's the same old story, a story as old as Christ.

Again, more thunder, lightning, rain. What a downpour!

* * *

Marie lives across the hall from Don Paul. She works at a video store and takes classes at the university. She's only seventeen. She has a lovely body and is aware of it. Her face is thin. Don Paul loves her dark questioning eyes and more than that. He's twice her age, but she likes him. She lends him books. Sometimes they go to a doughnut shop for coffee. Don Paul is thinking about her now because he can hear the key in the door across the hall. *Sweet Marie.* He likes to call her that because she comes on strong with hope, beaming goodwill. She wants to become a social worker. There is maybe a drop of one percent Canadian Indian in her, which for her is enough to save a whole nation.

The door. It's her. "Hello," Don Paul says, "I thought it was you." She is soaked from the rain. Her black eyes are flashing. She holds a bottle of dark red wine.

"I was hoping you might have a drink with me," she says. "I'm soaked to the skin." Her T-shirt is clinging to her well-developed breasts. Her nipples are taut, thimble-like, as if someone has suckled them. Don Paul wonders how they would feel between his own lips.

"A drink sounds good to me," he says. "Where's Fred?" (Fred being her latest boyfriend.)

"Oh, he's somewhere around I guess. We're not all that serious anymore. Why don't I dry off and change? Drop over in ten minutes, okay?" She smiles. She giggles. What innocence. Don Paul finds it frightening the way her young body swims at him, splashing teasing tickles through his groin. *So kind. She is so kind.* She looks for something good in everybody. She even wants to save the seals.

"Okay," he says, "I'll be over." She smiles again. Strands of long wet hair cling to her bone-smooth cheeks. *Does she fantasize like I do?* He imagines the hard time she's going to have pulling off her tight jeans, her wet T-shirt. He feels hard. But he'll do no wrong. Before going to Marie's, he'll take care of the hardness himself.

* * *

Inside Marie's room, which is not much larger than his own, Don Paul flops down on the sofa and watches as she pours the wine. She has a different T-shirt on now. Her hard nipples have behaved like shy snails and have all but disappeared. And now, instead of tight jeans, she is wearing a loose-fitting pair of grey slacks. He feels very relaxed. The wine is poured. Humming sweetly, she slips down beside him, close enough to touch his arm. If he made a move? Dare he make a move? What would she do? Would she welcome it? If she did, what then? Would he be cursed with some lasting commitment? Probably not.

She leans into him. She crosses her legs and dangles a bare foot. So natural, always teasing. "It's so stuffy in here," she says, and sips her wine. "These rooms are terrible. Slum landlords, I hate them. What did you do all day?" Her hand gives his knee a playful tap.

"Very little," Don Paul replies. "I went to the store and bought some fruit and cereal, came home and watched the storm. I like the sound of thunder. The lightning flashing, the way it scares people."

"Yeah, I really got soaked," Marie says. "The weather is awful. Look at my hair." She lifts a strand to show Don Paul what a tangle it is. He smiles at her childlike behaviour. He can smell her wet hair. It smells good, like some kind of strange new and wild animal. He has thoughts of taming her.

"You should do something, Don. You can't sit around here and do nothing all your life."

"Oh?"

"Well, it's not healthy. Maybe you're rich enough that you don't have to work, but don't you want more? Something better, nicer?"

"I really don't think so. I'm not fussy. My needs are few. Perhaps it'd be different if I had a family, then I'd have to be responsible, be a provider of sorts, but I'm all alone, you see. And to tell you the truth, most of the time I prefer it that way."

"Why?" Marie asks. "It's no good to live alone. It's not natural. And you lie if you say that you feel all right about it.

People need people. People need to be active. You said you once worked, took odd jobs, worked hard too, you say. What changed you?"

"I don't know. Somewhere along the line, I just got too tired—fed up. I asked questions. I didn't get answers. I don't know. Nothing seems to make sense. Maybe it's just a stage I'm going through, but then, it might be something else. All I see these days is pain, suffering, and the ones that aren't suffering don't think."

"I'm not suffering."

"It's like a poison. And so, I say, that's it, that's enough. The hell with it. Count me out."

Marie jumps up. "How about supper? Why don't you stay for supper? I'm making spaghetti. Afterwards, we'll talk about your future. I have something that I want you to try out, an experiment, a remedy, something to make you feel better, something that might get rid of the toxins churning inside your mind and body. Maybe you'll get an appetite for life. That's what you need, Don Paul, an appetite for living, some kind of antitoxin."

2

The experiment is a job, volunteer work. Marie wants Don Paul to get involved with a senior citizen, become a friend to a man in his seventies. While doing a practicum for her social work class, she has visited an old boy by the name of Roy Templeton, a shut-in who, she says, enjoys chess. "Right away," Marie says, "when he mentioned the game, I thought about you. Remember trying to teach me how to play?"

"Hey, wait a minute, I'm no expert. I enjoy a game now and then, but that's all."

"I know. He's the same way too," Marie says. "It's no big deal. Just go there and visit, maybe once a week, have a game, then say goodbye. No fuss. It's what you need—a person in your life outside of this grubby rooming-house.

You'll do the both of you a favour. Come on, whadaya say? Bring some joy into the old boy's life. It'll do you a world of good too."

Marie won't let up on how wonderful the experience would be. How grateful she would be to Don if he decided to take the job. She keeps on and on about it, growing more and more excited. And, while she speaks, she nonchalantly brushes against Don Paul's bare arm. He thinks of not giving in, if only to find out how far she might be willing to go. When Marie gets fired up on one of her good causes, pleading and squirming the way she does, you can feel her energy run right through you. He fights with himself. He wants to stop what's on his mind. Like the other day, there was a young girl on the street in a pretty pink dress. She had lovely shaped legs and small budding breasts. Oh, how he had to turn away. Oh, how he had to stop himself from looking, sensing that he desired to reach out and feel her newness. And with Marie, his thoughts are much the same. He could easily be her professor, her father, or any one of a number of dirty old men. But he isn't, he's Don Paul, a man who can't let reason escape for a minute, because all will be lost. He knows he's walking a thin line and one step beyond that line could mean the madhouse! No, better not to move at all, better to pretend, better to think everything and believe nothing. Better to dream. Better to make sure you know you're dreaming. *Yes, for God's sake, make sure you know the difference!*

Don Paul leaves Marie content with the idea that she has sucked him into becoming a volunteer. He can picture her bragging about it to her classmates tonight. The professor will probably give her a B+. But maybe playing the good Samaritan for a while is what he needs. After all, if he doesn't like the old boy, there's no law says he has to see the old guy again.

* * *

Lately, Don Paul has not been sleeping well. Tonight is no exception. The humidity seems to steam from the night, from the air in his room, but in fact it's rising up from the wet streets. Along with it comes the returning fantasy of wanting to make love to young Marie.

Today's rain has raised the heat off the pavement and it has entered his room. He wonders about buying a fan. Every summer Don Paul plans on buying a fan but never does. Instead, he lies naked and dreams of cooler nights. Eventually, they arrive. Eventually, the sweating stops, but that happy medium doesn't last long. Soon, Don Paul paces the room, cursing the landlord for raising the rent but never the heat. He thinks Marie might be right. He should change his situation: work, increase his income, move into a modern apartment. But it's easier to complain, to have the environment parallel his dark thoughts. Besides, no matter how or where he lives, his view of the world is not likely to change. The negative side to Don Paul was fixed in his youth where, so long ago, he was subjected to a rude awakening, a happening that started fears and questions at an early age. Don Paul fell, fell hard. He landed on the dark side, the outside, and ever since could only look in.

He was seven years old. His father had bought a small cottage in the Laurentian Mountains, an hour's drive north of Montreal. And, at first, in the mornings, when sun shone through Don Paul's bedroom window, there was no moaning or groaning. No need to yell out to his mother, "Okay, okay, just give me another minute." For all that first week in his home away from home, as soon as his eyelids fluttered open he leaped out of bed. Summer was here. The countryside was alive and waiting and nobody had to coax him up for that. Don Paul spent a lot of time at a bridge, at a story-book setting, a swimming hole where the sun's rays reflected off the water, and he could see the bottom where sunfish, shiners and perch were swimming. On one particular morning, he leaned over the rail and spat. He listened to his phlegm slap the surface; it wasn't that far, but the gap between water and bridge echoed the sound. And as he watched the phlegm float, drift, then dissipate downstream, he heard a sound, some bit of music, like a mouth organ. Birds stopped singing. Some flew away. The music continued. It was a familiar tune, "Red River Valley," and the sound seemed to be coming from inside the woods, on his left, not far from the creek. The music grew louder, closer. Don Paul tried to imagine who it might be. As far as he knew, there were no cottages near the water, no cars parked on the road. It was too early for anyone to go swimming. He walked further along, close to the railing, squinting, searching, but there was nothing to see except more trees, more green bushes. Then the sound stopped and he waited; he could hear nothing but his own breathing and, except for the odd minnow rippling the surface of the water, it seemed as if the whole world waited with him. Then, some bushes moved. He heard voices. Two boys older than himself stepped out of the woods. Their jeans were held up with red suspenders. They wore checked shirts, and they had black and white running shoes on their feet. Farm boys.

"Who's you up there?" one of them called.

"My name's Don Paul," he called down. He was relieved to hear that his voice didn't break.

"Where do you live?" asked the other boy.

"Most of the time in the city," said Don Paul. "My father bought a country home not far from here."

One boy turned to the other and he seemed to be whispering something. "We've just been out to have a look around," the taller one said, suppressing laughter. "Why don't you come down here and see what we've found?" And they put their hands over their mouths, snickering.

Because Don Paul was anxious to make friends, he agreed to see what they were up to. Trying his best not to show how uneasy and fearful he felt, he walked down and stood beside them in the little clearing. With no further introduction, they led him over to a narrow path that ran into the woods. As soon as Don Paul had entered, he regretted his position in the middle, the tall one giggling to himself close behind him. If he had to run, there would be no means of escape. No sooner was Don Paul mulling over that fear than the boy behind shouted, "Now get him, Harry!" And before Don Paul could turn around, Harry's long arm had come up and caught Don in a headlock. Like a bulldogger at a rodeo, he hauled Don Paul along a few steps, then they pushed him down into a shallow hole. It must have been recently dug, for at the same moment, as he was being pushed in, Don Paul caught a glimpse of a spade sticking upright in the sand.

Kneeling there, sun in his eyes, with those two goofy faces peering down at him, he said in his bravest voice, "This is a stupid trick! I want out of here!" And as Don Paul started to crawl, it hit him: a putrid odour, an odour so indescribably strong that all the air around him was sick with it. And to Don Paul's disbelief, the younger boy took hold of the shovel and stuck the flat blade hard against Don's chest.

"No, no . . . you stay right there," he warned. "Stay, until we're good and ready to let you up."

"Yeah," the older boy said. "Close the dog's eyes, then maybe we'll think about letting you go."

There was a dog there all right, in the hole to the left of him. The animal was curled in the corner. The stomach was split, exposing a wide line of dried blood, and hundreds and hundreds of white things were crawling all over the dark decomposing stink. It was later on that Don Paul found out that what were crawling were maggots, for he had previously shown little interest as to what went on beneath his feet. As a matter of fact, the dog was Don Paul's first encounter with something so large that was dead.

"Shut his eyes for us," the boy ordered again, the shovel pressing hard against Don Paul's side.

"What for?" he managed to say. His mind was dizzy with fright, the steel blade hurting.

"Shut his eyes," the boy repeated. "We want to bury him, stupid. Wouldn't be right to shovel dirt in poor old Sandy's eyes, even if he is dead. Hit by a car. Maybe it was your father's car?"

"No, we didn't hit anything," Don Paul said and gagged, hardly aware that he had spoken. He was out of it, lost in fear, lost in that strange secretive insect world where the body of an animal becomes a home in which to live and breed. He knew that the maggots could not be conscious of the dog's mouth as being a mouth, nor of the nose as being a nose. Yet, he had an awful rot-gut feeling that those creatures sensed they had a large chunk of edible substance which offered strange new beginnings. He was aware that the maggots were using the gaping mouth as an entrance to everything hidden below, while the nostrils, he supposed, were tunnel-like vents to the brain. The idea that anything so smelly and gruesome could really exist in the world left Don Paul more afraid of death than of the human threats.

Again, one of the boys shouted down for him to shut the dog's eyes—"or else!" The spell was broken. He was out of the maggot world, back in their world, and both were too much for him to bear. He screamed. He screamed so long and hard and loud that the boys jumped backwards, which gave Don Paul enough time and room to leap out. He was still screaming too, screaming all the way along the path, then down the road. His sounds were so disturbing that the boys did not give chase. *Home!* As soon as Don Paul's mother opened the door, he flew into her arms. He told his parents that some big fellows were after him and that he'd rather live in the city again. That night, the nightmares began. For the first week, almost every night. Then, after the family had returned to the city, there was at least one terrible dream every second week. Mother would come into Don Paul's room and wake him, or he'd be awake, sitting up in bed trembling and so sweat-soaked that she would have to bring him a change of pyjamas. She called in a doctor. The doctor said there was nothing abnormal about Don Paul's behaviour. It was all part of growing up, he said. This diagnosis was not reassuring to Don Paul. The doctor's words, kindly meant, left Don Paul with a sense of dread, thinking this was the beginning of more horrors to come. Indeed, there were more horrors of a kind but, as far as he was concerned, they were never quite as bad as being held prisoner in a grave with a rotting maggot-infested dog. The smell and sight of those maggots feasting on that animal triggered a gradual distancing. Of course, being so young at the time, the boy's appetite for life did grow but, nevertheless, there was always that sensation, like a shadow, either in front or behind; and, at times, a voice from deep within taunted him. "Give it up," it would say. "Give it up!"

3

Early the next morning, Marie sees Don Paul and tells him where Roy Templeton lives. And while she is speaking with Don Paul at the door, he takes all of her in. She is wearing a short summer dress.

"Does he have a chess game?" Don Paul suddenly asks, hoping to erase what he is thinking about Marie.

"No, you better bring yours. I phoned him. He knows you're coming."

"What time?"

"I said anytime today. I want you to know that I really appreciate what you're doing, Don. I'm sure that the two of you will like one another. Here's his address." She hands him a slip of pink paper. "I've gotta run. I'm late for work." Before leaving, Marie surprises Don Paul by giving him a quick peck on the cheek. As he reads the note, Don Paul's fingers touch where she has kissed his unshaved skin. It is the first time he has ever felt her lips. The kiss makes him smile. He thinks

Marie would make a fine doctor; he can barely understand what she has written.

Sticking the note in his pants pocket, Don Paul decides to visit Templeton after lunch. If the name of the street is correct, Templeton is only a short bus ride away. Don Paul is sure that the number is a senior citizens' apartment building. Since he's been awake for more than two hours, his stomach feels lax, sour again. It has a nauseating, seasick queasy roll to it, reminding Don Paul of a ferry ride he once took to Prince Edward Island. Paper bags were handed to everyone, and as bad as Don Paul's stomach churned, oddly he was one of the few who didn't throw up. This sick feeling has been with Don Paul for so long now, he's convinced his body has accepted the queasiness as normal. Nevertheless, although there is no hint of an appetite today, he'll try to get something down. He's afraid that if he gets too tired and weak he might fall down or faint, which, touch wood, so far has never happened.

* * *

There are three rooms in the house and the landlord lives downstairs. Besides Marie and himself, there is a man at the end of the hall who calls himself Mac. Don Paul does not see Mac very often. Mac sleeps most of the day—works at night somewhere, maybe as a security guard. While Don Paul is on his way out, Mac is on his way in. They meet on the stairs.

"Wait a minute," Mac says. "That's bad luck."

"What's bad luck?" Don Paul asks.

"Passing a person on the stair. Wait until I come up."

Don Paul steps back to let Mac through. Mac is a big man with a wide smile. He looks like a good beer drinker. He often smells like one. It is early. Right now Mac looks sober. But with people like Mac you can never tell.

Mac reaches the top of the stairs and stands beside Don Paul. Mac is breathing like a wounded bull. He smells sweet with aftershave. Don Paul counts five blade nicks on Mac's fat face and thick red neck. Mac has a newspaper with him. He thrusts the newspaper in front of Don Paul. A chubby finger points to what Don Paul should read. "What do you think of that?" he asks. Don Paul's eyes focus on a short article proclaiming that in the United States alone last year, over thirteen hundred children, people under the age of eighteen, were charged with murder. Kids as young as five years old had killed their playmates. "That's not the kind of world I grew up in," Mac says, shaking his head, and without saying another word sways down the hallway and enters his room.

On his way downstairs, Don Paul thinks about the article. It seems so unreal, something made up just to shock people, but that's unlikely. *Thirteen hundred kids.* What a horror story! The figures boggle the mind. On the way to Roy Templeton's place, sitting on the bus, the numbers are still in his head. What are they doing? Do they shoot one another and then go home for cartoons and peanut butter and jam?

Through the bus window, Don Paul spots some children running wild in the schoolyard. What lesson have they learned today? Maybe some boy has learned how to kick another in the head. Yes, boots to the head. *Apes?* Don Paul thinks. Worse than apes! *Violence.* Everywhere there's violence. Show me children. Show me those childlike eyes. Show me the beautiful blues, browns and greens. *Children*, how smooth the word. How coarse the little people have become. And the mother sings: "No, no, not my Johnny. My Johnny's good! Johnny wouldn't hurt a soul."

"Well then, madam, tell him to put the fuckin' gun away."

The bus passes the schoolyard. Don Paul takes one last look and mumbles, "Children." *Over thirteen hundred. Murderers.* The exact figure, what was it? Thirteen hundred and eleven. And since the article was written, the killings have, no doubt, increased in number. How do you try to understand something like that?

Don Paul guessed right about Templeton's place being an

apartment building for seniors. Two old men and three ladies are sitting outside waiting for . . . *what? Who wants to think about what they're waiting for?* Roy Templeton is on the third floor, number 302. There are more seniors in the lobby waiting for the mailman to finish sorting. The one winter that Don Paul worked as a letter carrier, the seniors in apartments were all the same, meeting in lobbies, rustling about like clusters of dried leaves, chatting to one another about the news and the weather and, at the same time, always watchful to see who got what and jealous when one received more than another. Like children, so hungry for love.

What a strange feeling to see the people and their mail again. It's been years. They see him. He smiles and nods.

"Are you the doctor?" one of them asks.

"No," Don Paul replies, "just visiting a friend."

"It's the doctor," another one says.

"Ohoooo," a woman moans, "who's sick?"

"Nobody," Don Paul says, then realizes what has happened: they have mistaken his black chess box for a medical kit. And he is also wearing white slacks. "It must be Mr. Wilson," a quavering voice says. Don Paul steps into the elevator. "He's been sick for months. But that's not his regular doctor, is it? No, no, that's not Dr. Chung." Before the elevator door closes, Don Paul nods again. Their eyes look tired, kind, and helpless. *They're the little children, the real children.* He wonders if he'll last long enough to live in one of these places. Maybe it's not so bad. You get meals. And if you feel like talking, well, you can have a chat with someone when the mail comes.

On the third floor, the hall is deserted. The air smells of rubbing alcohol. Don Paul feels sure that everyone here is on some kind of medication. He knocks on Roy Templeton's door. All is quiet. The dot of light from the peephole disappears.

"Yes," a voice whispers.

"It's me, Mr. Templeton. Don Paul, Marie's friend. I've come over for a game of chess." The chain clicks off the lock. The door opens to reveal a frail-looking man with clear suspicious eyes. "Hi," Don Paul says. "Marie said she phoned you."

"Yes, that's right. Here—come in." He points a long shaky finger at the small living room. "Sit down in there, if you like. I'll make us some tea. Or would you rather set the game up in the kitchen?"

"Maybe that would be best," Don Paul says. "Better to sit straight up to play chess."

Don Paul stands near the entrance of the kitchen, waiting for Roy to clear the table. It looks as if he has just finished lunch. The apartment is not much bigger than Don Paul's one room, except Roy Templeton has his own washroom, whereas Marie, Mac and Don share the one bathroom in the hall.

Roy Templeton has something in every corner, things he probably couldn't bring himself to part with. There are too many end tables and small chairs. Cardboard boxes are piled on top of one another. Some are filled with books. There are heaps of clothing, pots and pans scattered helter-skelter on the floor. A pole-lamp stands beside the door next to a big green plastic frog. The frog's back is open. Don Paul guesses it's made to hold umbrellas or canes. But instead of anything like that, he spies a giant-size box of Tide soap inside. He also notices that there are no pictures on the walls. "I just moved in a week ago. In fact, Marie found this place for me. Just can't find the energy to put much away. First move in thirty-eight years. Wife died last year and I finally sold the house. Guess this is my last chapter. Maybe it's best to have it end this way." Roy plugs in the kettle and drops a teabag into a dark brown teapot.

Don Paul does not know how to answer the old man. He begins to set up the chess pieces. Roy comes near to help, but forgets on what square the queen goes. "Queen on her own colour," Don Paul says. "You'll always get it right then." The old man frowns. Don Paul bites his lower lip; he's made it sound as if Roy doesn't know what he is doing. Well, he doesn't, does he? thinks Don Paul. But he lets Roy have the white pieces, a gesture of goodwill. White moves first. Shaky fingers move a pawn.

"It's been years since I played this game," Roy says. "Do you play often?"

"No, not very often," says Don Paul. He studies the board. "Don't know many that do, personally that is. I haven't played chess for years either. Marie never did show much interest in the game. Too slow, she said. Makes me sleepy, she said. Sometimes I play a tournament game out of the newspaper, but the last real game must have been with a friend more than twenty years ago."

After the second chess move, Roy Templeton gets up to pour the tea. Don Paul can tell that this will be a long game, and a long day. Tea poured, Roy looks for his pipe which, when found and filled and lit, throws him into a fit of coughing. He leans over the kitchen sink. He turns the water on and hacks into the flow. While he's doing this, Don Paul silently curses Roy for using the sink and not the washroom. "You okay?" Don Paul asks.

The coughing slows and Roy turns the water off. "Happens all the time," he says. "Hard to give up old habits."

Finally, when they're about to resume play, the old man, without even batting an eye, breaks wind. And while the air around Don Paul dies, traps him, he finds himself also caught in an awkward moment of silence. He watches Roy study the board. Don Paul is sure Roy Templeton doesn't give a damn about what he's done. Then, with watery eyes, Roy stares at Don Paul and says, "Did you want it *tore* like that, or all in one piece?" Don Paul holds his nose and laughs. Don Paul thinks that Roy is a real vulgar old goat of a man, but an honest old goat.

They play like amateurs: better moves are noticed after silly ones are made. An hour later, Don Paul is ahead a knight and two pawns. Not long afterwards, Roy loses interest. He begins to talk about old times: his life on the farm and working on the railroad. For Don Paul it's all pretty boring, but he can tell that Roy likes talking about it, so he listens. Roy's voice rises and his eyes light up with memories. Don Paul feels sure that there will be no ending the game today. He suggests that they call "time" and resume play the following week. Roy agrees. "Do you want to keep this one going?" asks Don Paul. "Or start fresh when we meet again?"

"Maybe we'll start fresh," Roy says. "Right now, I think that I better have a lay-down. I always have a little lay-down in the afternoon."

"That's fine with me," says Don Paul and is relieved to hear it. He does not have to make up some excuse to leave. He puts the chessmen into the box and folds the board.

"What do you do?" Roy asks Don Paul at the door.

"At this moment," says Don, "I have no career. I used to work odd jobs, but since my father's death, I've done very little. Do you think that's wrong? Marie does."

Roy rubs his chin. "I don't know. Maybe you're just plain lazy, but then again, who's to say what's what about who today?" He shakes Don Paul's hand hard, as if to let him know there's still some life left. "If you come next week, maybe we'll forget about the game and have a chat instead. Maybe I'll have this place in order by then."

"Fine. I'll give you a call, but if you don't feel up to it, don't hesitate to let me know."

With his chessmen under his arm, Don Paul has that after-Sunday-School feeling: he had always hated to go to church, but felt good once it was over. For a while, Don Paul thought of the good feeling as some kind of spiritual renewal. But then he concluded it was all psychological. Whatever it was, he felt good about himself and feels that way now. His step is light. He taps his chessmen box and tells the old girl standing near the front door that Mr. Wilson is fine and should live to be at least ninety-nine. "Oh, that's wonderful," she replies. "I don't know what we'd ever do without such good service as yours, Doctor."

4

There seemed to be no reason for Don Paul to tell Roy Templeton that he usually had an afternoon lay-down as well. But this late in the day, with the sun hitting his side of the building full force, Don Paul finds it too difficult to sleep. Something has to be done to alleviate the heat. He decides not to put it off any longer; he'll buy a fan. A small one to put on the window-sill. Maybe I'm losing my mind, thinks Don Paul, for the idea of making the purchase comes to him as some big project to work out. It all has to be planned: his getting up, his dressing, his going to the store, the time of day he goes. *Should it be before or after supper?* "So much to consider," says Don Paul. "So much to make me crazy." He stares at the high, yellow, paint-chipped ceiling. "I need to relax. Get my thoughts in their right order. Being conscious of *being* is what rattles the brain. Maybe that's why work is so necessary, to stop a person from thinking about their dry existence."

Don Paul falls in and out of sleep. He sees that dog again, the one with the maggots; then he thinks about another dead animal, the deer that Don Paul's father had in his half-ton truck. Don Paul couldn't understand why his father and his father's friends were so pleased at having such a beautiful creature dead. Voices were rattling. One man used the tip of his long rifle barrel to point at the two different spots where the bullets had entered. Blood on the animal looked thick and sticky. Most of it had run down the left front leg. One big drop had jelled, and hung from a blood string that dangled from a hoof. To Don Paul, deer didn't look like wild creatures. They looked more like large gentle pets.

The hunters had argued about whose shot made the kill.

A hunter with dirty hands rubbed Don Paul's head. Another hunter waved his hat in the air and let out a loud hoot. Don Paul's father sent Don Paul into the cottage to get each of his hunter friends another beer. Don Paul's mother looked unhappy. Don Paul doesn't remember much after that except that he heard a lot of loud voices and loud songs. And when his mother tucked him into bed that night she told him not to get up for anything, except if he had to go to the bathroom. She said he was to call her and that she would come to take him. The toilet was outside. He remembers that he later woke up with a start and he thought he heard his mother crying somewhere. The bed felt wet.

Don Paul doesn't hate hunters. He was a hunter himself: killed birds and rabbits, but never a deer. There is something about a deer. Innocence. Beauty. What people find appealing. What people feel compelled to destroy. "Hey," Don Paul says to himself. "Have you ever been so mad that you wanted to club a baby seal? That's a good one. I'll tell Marie that one. Hey, Sweet Marie, I felt so crazy-mad today that I wanted to club a baby seal! Enough. I must get dressed—buy that fan."

It's upsetting; he feels so simple-minded about it. A simple decision ought not to be so troublesome but, like the food, only certain things are allowed to go down, and in this case only certain things are allowed to come in, become fixed in his small space. For, unlike Roy Templeton, Don Paul refuses to let his room become a crammed den of odds and ends. That fan will be his biggest purchase of the year. And he has made a rule: if something comes in, something goes out. But what? Right now everything seems so necessary. Maybe there's something in the kitchen he hasn't used very often. He shakes his head. "Don Paul, you're never going to understand yourself. But don't give up," he says. "Promise yourself that."

* * *

He frowns at the price and hands over his card. Like everyone else, Don Paul buys with a plastic card. He knows that businessmen have great money-making minds, realizing that people generally buy a lot more junk with a card. People just say, "Charge it!" As Don Paul is doing now—disturbed that he too has fallen into the trap, accepting whatever the entrepreneurs have to offer, as if a person can't get along without doing it their way. But he'll never conform to the dogma that more of everything is better. He thinks more of himself than that. There are things he can cut out, do without, but not the fan, not today. He needs the fan.

With his fan in a box and his box in a bag and the bag under his arm, Don Paul takes long strides, anxious to be home, to plug the thing in.

The streets are dirty, dusty; bits of paper stick flat in the gutter. He hears a crash. He grips the fan tight under his arm. One car has hit another. A door opens. Don Paul sees the driver, an old man. The man leans out. He falls into the street. He rolls once, twice. He rolls like a long log. He moans. He groans. People run to him. The driver from the other car leaps out and runs to him. Don Paul wants to run to him too, but can't—won't—move. *Everything should be all right.* There are plenty of people around already, although he could have—should have—been the first there.

"What happened?" a woman asks. She is loaded down with groceries. Two small children cling tight to her heavy legs. Don Paul notices how dark and puffy her eyes look. Every day must be a struggle for her, although Don Paul feels she doesn't see it that way. "There's been an accident," he tells her. He hears an ambulance scream, sees a flashing red light coming. The woman's face is blank, as if she's waiting for a movie to begin. It's running, he wants to say. It's running right in front of you. Can't you see it? She turns with the kids still tight on her legs. They go and Don Paul goes too, walking and thinking about how the world will stop to let people through, like the ambulance drivers. The doctors. *Oh doctor, right this way. Please let the medicine man through.* Let him come through to take something out, seal your skin, sew you up, hopefully without pain, and always, whether you live or die, without remorse. Don Paul once heard a man say, "In the bad hospitals they let you die, and in the good ones they kill you." Don Paul is sure that is true. His father was in a *good* hospital. *How are they trained?* Is there a special course for medical students, perhaps the clergy too, on how to keep a straight face when confronted with all that blind faith, the trust so many people put in such well-paid jerks? "Oh, how easy it is to be fooled." Don Paul rubs his temples. There is no pain, only the thinking. He uses his fingers to massage the side of his head because his mind spins with some strange new lucidity.

* * *

The fan works fine. He lies on his bed and lets the air wash him, bless him. The air feels good, like life breathing over him. The house is quiet. Marie is at work. Mac is either at the bar or sleeping one off. Bob Benson, the landlord, leaves early and comes home late. He keeps to himself and doesn't say much unless you're late with the rent. Anyway, that's what Marie tells Don Paul. For his own rent, Don Paul has given the landlord a year of post-dated cheques; he has no need to speak with the man. But if Don Paul happens to spot another mouse running around, he's going to say something quick. It has taken Don Paul a long time to get used to the one mouse he has and that one is more than enough. He calls the little fellow Rambo and feeds him potato chips.

5

Don Paul is not quite sure, but he thinks he must have seen Roy Templeton at least eight times all in one month. Today, Marie comes into Don Paul's room to inform him that Roy is dead. "He died in his sleep last night," she says. "I'm sorry for you, Don Paul. You were beginning to like him, weren't you?"

"Beginning to like him?" Don Paul says. "Yes, as old and as crude as he was, I liked him. I must admit, I think it was because of him I was beginning to feel better. I had developed some routine, some interest in someone outside of myself. I was eating better too." He looks away from Marie's stare. Her eyes look too sharp for the moment. He suddenly feels tired, very tired. He walks to his bed and sits down. Marie comes to him. She sits next to him on the bed and places her hand on his. Don Paul cannot help but smile and admire how sweet and kind and natural she becomes at easing life's woes. He puts his arm around her and kisses her on the cheek. She turns her face and kisses him on the mouth. Her tongue presses in. As nice as this feels and although it stirs him, Don Paul pulls back and whispers that he needs some time alone. "I understand," Marie says. "Maybe we can go for a walk later—have a coffee."

"Are you planning to go to school tonight?"

"No, not tonight. If you need me, I'll be in my room. The funeral is Wednesday. We'll go together."

"Yes," Don Paul says, allowing himself to fall flat on the bed, locking his fingers and cupping both hands behind his head. "I would like that. I mean the both of us going together."

With Marie gone, Don Paul closes his eyes. He is aware of the fan humming, the cars passing outside the window. The sounds take him to a little waterfall flowing down a mountain-side, near a place called Weir, Quebec. His grandparents retired there. Before his folks bought a cottage in the same area, his father and mother would drive him up and leave him with his grandparents on weekends and school holidays. He loved the nights, with his bedroom window open, and Grandmother would spread her thick down-filled quilts on top of his thin body. He felt warm and happy in the big wooden bed. And the rhythm of the falls. And the sound of the night birds, like that of the whippoorwill, would lull Don Paul into the deepest of sleeps, where his dreams were cloud-filled hills bathed in soft yellow light. Come morning, Don Paul would awaken to the sounds and smells of bacon frying on top of the crackling wood-burning stove. His hours were filled with sights and sounds he never wanted to lose. Yes, those times, those nights, they were all taken for granted, and to have one return, wouldn't that be the greatest of things? That, Don Paul imagines, would be a true miracle. But would it be enough of a miracle to restore his faith in mankind?

* * *

Wednesday. Don Paul dresses early. He is prepared to call on Marie. He knows that Roy had a son and daughter. He should be able to recognize them from the photographs Roy showed him. If they are there, Don Paul plans to do the expected, to shake hands, to tell them how sorry he is. The daughter will probably shed a tear. The son will probably put on his best sad face. Don Paul will feel sorry for them, or pretend to be. As far as he knows, they haven't been to visit their father for years.

With his tie straight, Don Paul leaves his room and knocks on Marie's door. Marie calls out for him to come in. He can't get over how lovely she looks. She looks like she is dressed for a party. Marie races downstairs and waits for Don Paul at the bottom. "Come on, you slowpoke," she calls. She smiles and swings the front door open. Down on the sidewalk, she slips her arm through his.

"When the funeral is over we're going to his daughter's for drinks," Marie says.

"Oh?" Don Paul says, suddenly surprised and irritated. The heat from the street and her cheery voice hang on him like a rope around his neck. He can hardly breathe. *The day grows so warm so fast.* The air, his stomach, it all feels like poison. While they're waiting for the bus to take them to church, Don Paul has a strong urge to run away from Marie, away from the street, away from the city too. He wishes to be in his room packing clothes, getting ready to leave for no place in particular. Who will he know at the funeral anyway? Nobody. "I'm not going!" Don Paul blurts out. "I want no part of it."

"What?"

"I say, I'm not going to the funeral. I don't feel up to going."

"Not up to going?" Marie says, narrowing her eyes at him. "You don't feel up to going? Who does? Nobody feels up to going to a funeral. It's just something you have to do, that's all." She lets his arm go. She steps in front of him. Faces him. "You have to go," she says. "It's all so very necessary—you, me, we are expected to be there. What do I say to people when they want to know where you are?"

"What people? I don't know anybody!"

The tears she has held for the funeral pour out.

"I'm sorry," Don Paul says, not caring. "Catch you later. Tell me how it went."

"Tell you how it went?" She stammers, "Why—why should I tell you anything? I think you're dreadful. I think you're selfish and mean!"

"I think so too," says Don Paul, and he leaves Marie standing at the bus stop.

* * *

Was it all a mistake? he asks himself. Getting close to an older person, when you know some day they won't be there and you will. No, Don Paul believes that's all right. There are certain things you don't want to consider in terms of the end result. The death of a person, no matter how old he is, is one of them.

His tie chokes him. He pulls it off. There has been a real heat wave and maybe it was the heat that killed Roy. Come to think of it, Don Paul does not remember ever seeing a fan at Roy Templeton's place and it got pretty stuffy in there. If I would have bought him one? Maybe he would be alive and kicking today. No, most likely not. I don't think he would've plugged it in. *The stupid old fart.*

Don Paul does not go right home. He finds himself heading into a park, seeking a bench and a shade tree. He is not far away from the street's traffic.

Cities have a way of working on you, thinks Don Paul. They drain you, leave you drooping like the wilted leaves. He sits and watches and thinks about the tall trees, their dryness, their silent cries for rain. He envies the trees. They need only sun and rain and their lives will be rich and full. *It's people, the ones who think, they suffer.*

Don Paul closes his eyes. The light dims. The brightness is replaced with white and pink dots, odd pictures, an empty landscape, strange faces. Then a shadow disturbs the little light he still sees. "Do you know where the pigeons are?" The voice belongs to a thin woman with a cane. She is wearing a large straw hat and blue dress. She looks like an American, some southern belle out of *Gone with the Wind.* Instead of a purse, she carries a shopping bag on her arm. Don Paul concludes that she must be in her eighties. He cannot understand why she is out in such terrible heat.

"The pigeons?" he repeats, not feeling fully awake. "There are no pigeons. They've brought in some kind of hawks or falcons to kill them off. They said we had too many."

Her eyes glisten teary blue. "I used to feed them," she says, and lifts the bag a little. "I know they're messy useless things, but I like them. Do you think hawks have killed them all?"

"No, I'm sure the birds just flew off to a better place, somewhere safe."

"Well," she says, leaving the concrete path and stepping onto the grass, "I'll just set these crumbs out for the squirrels then."

Don Paul turns and watches as she tilts her shopping bag to dump a heap of what appear to be cookies and bread crumbs onto the grass. She glances his way. She waves and smiles, then shuffles off toward the street. Don Paul considers the mess she's made. He believes no squirrels will come to eat the crumbs. He wonders if she knows that too.

Don Paul gets up to leave. His mind moves as quickly as his footsteps. Roy Templeton must be in the ground by now. Marie will be having some wine and cheese. There will be talk about what a wonderful man Roy was, how much he'll be missed. Don Paul was his only visitor. Roy didn't mind closing the book. So Don Paul reasons that he shouldn't be too upset about Roy's going. It's the idea, he thinks. Death. It's what happens to you rather than to the person who no longer feels. It leaves you thinking about your own ending, about how natural it is to die and have everything continue on without you. And then—this heat! There is never enough right weather. With all the suffering, you'd think God would at least try to give us good weather. "Maybe he tries," says Don Paul, "tries and fails, tries and fails, over and over again. But then, then God . . . Oh, why should I think about God anyway?"

Don Paul considers his post-dated cheques, getting them back from the landlord. If he's going to be moving on, that's the first thing he'll have to do, in case his landlord tries to cash them in.

Don Paul looks across the street, between two tall buildings. His mouth opens and he stares, not moving. People stop to see where he is looking. Not seeing anything, they give up, shake their heads and continue along. Far off, between the two tall buildings, Don Paul studies a fine white line. It is nothing. It is only one lick of white light breaking through a piece of open sky.

A GREAT ARTIST

"I quit!"

"Nobody in their right mind quits school," the father said. "What happened?"

"I don't know what happened," said the boy. "I don't want to go back anymore, that's all."

"It's those paintings," his mother said. "Ever since he started painting, he's been acting peculiar. We've got to do something."

"We'll send him to a doctor."

The following week, the boy was taken to a doctor who had his practice in a spacious home in a well-to-do neighbourhood. As expected, there was a long black leather couch in the doctor's office. The boy asked if the doctor wanted him to lie down on the couch, but the doctor didn't think that would be necessary. Disappointed, the boy took a seat in one of the two matching black leather chairs.

The doctor said, "I want you to try and think of me as a friend. Do you think we might become friends?"

"Maybe," the boy said flatly and slouched in the chair. He wondered why the doctor needed a friend.

"The first thing I'd like to know is something about what you like to do. For instance, do you like sports?"

"Sports? No. I hate sports. I'm not one for joining in."

"What about hobbies? Do you have any hobbies?"

"Hobbies? Yes," the boy said, "I paint."

"*Paint?*" There was excitement in the doctor's voice. "What kind of painting? Oils? Watercolours?"

"Oils," said the boy. He stood up and moved around the room to look at some of the pictures hanging on the doctor's walls. There were many complex-looking drawings in India ink, and watercolours, and oils too, but nothing resembling what the boy liked to do.

"The pictures belong to patients of mine. I'd like to see some of your work too. Will you bring some in?"

"If you want," answered the boy, "I'll bring some in." He returned to his chair.

"Please now," the doctor said, "come and sit beside my desk. I want to give you some tests."

They were tests the boy had done in school: mathematics and something titled *What Words Are Spelled Funny?* And then two long pages of reading comprehension. The boy didn't care what kind of mark he got; he read and wrote quickly.

When he had finished, the doctor gathered up the papers and put them into a drawer. He asked the boy about school and teachers and what kind of friends he had, if any. The boy said he had no friends. The doctor nodded knowingly. He showed the boy a black and white photograph of a man standing in a dimly lit room. The man was looking out a window. There was nothing outside the window but a haze of white light. The doctor told the boy to look at the picture and make up a story. The boy handed the photograph back to the doctor. "I can't think of anything to say," he told him.

"Why not?" the doctor asked. "Can't you think of anything at all?"

"I can't think of anything at all."

The doctor looked at the picture, then glanced at his watch and yawned. As if speaking to himself, he said, "Okay then. That's fine then. That's enough for today."

The boy got up and followed the doctor to the door.

"Don't forget your paintings," the doctor said. "I'm anxious to see them."

Yeah, I bet, the boy thought to himself, but then he quickly said, "I'll bring some."

* * *

The following week, the boy brought six canvases.

One by one, the doctor looked at them, turning them this way and that. "This is the right side up," the boy informed him. "You've got that one upside-down."

"It doesn't matter," the doctor said. "I like them either way. I wonder, may I keep one of your paintings? For instance, this one? All these lines here, I think they're fascinating." The doctor ran his short stubby fingers over the dry rough lines.

"Shall I tell you how it's done?"

"No, no, there's no need for that," said the doctor.

"Why not?"

"I don't want to know, that's all. There's some structure, form, that's enough."

The boy couldn't understand why the doctor didn't want to know. After all, wasn't it his business to know why people did such things?

"I didn't use a brush," said the boy. "I took the tubes and squeezed the paint right out onto the canvas—"

"Ha, ha," the doctor laughed nervously. "Is that so? Well, well, what's say we find out about you in some other way? What's say we leave the paintings alone for now?"

The doctor stood the pictures up against the nearest wall and sat down in one of the black leather chairs. He looked exhausted. But the boy was determined to tell the man all he could.

"I want to talk about the painting," the boy said sharply. "I want to find out about myself."

"What?" said the doctor, sitting straight up in his chair as if he had been poked from underneath.

"The picture you want from me. I want to tell you how it was made. You see, I did it without a brush, without being careful, without being all that concerned whether one colour ran into the next. Does that make any sense to you?"

"What are you talking about? Sit down! You're getting yourself all worked up for nothing."

The boy had no thought of sitting down. He was anxious to hear himself. He went over to the wall and picked up the painting. "After I smeared the paint on," he said, "I took—"

"Never mind, never mind. Look, I'm sorry, but we must discuss something else—"

"I took the canvas and laid it on the floor—"

"No, no, I won't listen to that. I don't want to hear anything more about the paintings."

"I put them on the floor and then I—"

"I want you to stop. This kind of behaviour will get us nowhere. Please come and sit down."

"To get those lines that way," the boy said, watching the doctor make a face, "I stepped on the canvas. All those marks are my boot marks. What do you think of that? I tramped on my painting. Like this!" The boy began to stomp around the room. "Tramp! Tramp! Tramp!"

"Enough, enough!" cried the doctor. "There's no need to continue if you won't cooperate. I think you're deliberately trying to provoke me. I'm sorry, but I can't allow myself to play along. We'll have to see each other some other time. Out you go now. Go home and take a hot bath. Relax. That's what I'm going to do. Relax. Try and forget about painting for a while."

But the boy couldn't remember ever feeling so well; he told the doctor that everything was fine, that he had cured himself, and that some day he would become a great artist.

While gathering up his paintings, he asked the doctor if he still wanted one to keep. The doctor did not reply.

* * *

"You're early," the mother said. "What happened?"

"I'm finished," said the boy. "All the sessions are over with. Whatever it was, I'm cured. I'm going to go to school now."

"That's wonderful news. I knew a good doctor would do the trick. He probably said something we've been telling you for years, but I guess, like most, you've got to hear it from a professional."

"I know I have a lot to learn," he told his mother.

"What about your paintings? Did the doctor have anything to say about your paintings?"

"He liked them a lot," the boy said. "He wanted to buy one from me, but I said he couldn't have it at any price."

"*What?* He actually wanted to buy one of those awful things from you and you wouldn't sell it to him? I don't believe you. Which one was it?"

"This one!" said the boy, holding it up.

"Oh, how dreadful," the mother said, waving her arms. "Take it away. Take them all away. Put them in your room. Get them out of my sight!"

The boy stared at her; he giggled like a little girl. Then he gathered up his paintings. Going upstairs, he took two steps at a time. He walked down the hallway, unlocked a door, and entered his room.

THREE WORDS

The day you said "I love you," the day you put the ring on, how could you possibly know what heart-wrenching words would come, would spill from such a well-formed mouth? *How could you know?* In the beginning, hadn't she soaked up every touch? *Always.* What happened? One day in the kitchen, while she was drying the dishes beside the sink, you came in. And, like a dozen times before, you stepped in close behind her and wrapped your arms around her long smoothness and planted warm kisses on the back of her neck, then whispered, "I love you." *How could you know?* Not for one moment did you ever expect to be cut with such a sharp three-worded knife: *"Stop pawing me!"* From then on, it was as if somebody else had come to stay with you, somebody who was quite ill, so sick that both of you now walked around in silence, hardly breathing, let alone speaking, certainly never laughing, terrified of any utterances or anything mindful of what was so unbearable: *it is over.*

SHEEP IN THE FIELD

There were sheep in the field and the bus went by and the children cried, "Look! There's sheep in the field." And everyone strained to see. Even the old man on the grass-cutter turned his head and watched as the bus zoomed by with the sounds of "Sheep! Sheep!" screaming out the windows. Simultaneously, the sheep raised their heads, then, one by one, lowered them to graze again. A raven flew to another tree. And when the bus and the grass-cutter had gone by, a chipmunk broke its frozen stillness to do some nervous twitching, then scampered from a grassy knoll to the other side of the road. Sometimes other furry things would scamper across too. Occasionally, they wouldn't make it. Often they'd get squashed flat. Eventually, they'd look like old fish skins, black and dry and painted to the pavement.

* * *

Wendell Smith was walking along the boulevard, head down, books in hand, worrying, fretting about exams, when he spied one of the leaf-thin creatures that had not made it across in time. For some reason, maybe because of the bits of fur that were still visible, Wendell stopped thinking about exams. He reminisced about a large moose head which, years ago, hung on a wall in his uncle's cabin. When Wendell was a small boy, he used to ask his father to lift him up so he could pet the moose's nose. "Poor moose," Wendell would say, "poor moose." The head, especially the eyes, looked real, alive, too alive to be watching the world from a cabin wall, thought Wendell. "*Moose*," Wendell said, "I can't spend another minute dreaming about old moose heads." It was exam time; he had to concentrate on storing a sky-high mountain of facts inside his head.

* * *

Roxanne Rousseau, books cradled in one arm, walked a short distance behind Wendell. She saw the sheep in the field too. She thought they looked cute, happy: fluffy things without cares. She looked at the sky and admired the blue; she felt sure of herself and life, with a sense of belonging. Maybe it was the weather? The day seemed new, exciting, extremely bright, hot too. *Reality*, she thought. How wonderful it is to be high on reality. And she watched on the boulevard the row of trees that had been planted in honour of a group of Canadian soldiers who had been killed in a war some seventy-odd years ago. Roxanne liked the way the trees stood, very straight, tall and still, very much like soldiers. There was that fresh-cut grass smell in the air too, which, hard to know why, made her think about her boyfriend, Frank, who had first made love to her, in her mother's car, this year, in the back seat, on the first day of spring. The car was uncomfortably cold, but Roxanne liked the way Frank had done it to her. Well, eventually the way he had done it to her. He was so shy and awkward that she had to help him take his pants off. It was funny to think about it now, having to undress him. The memory suddenly sent a delightful chill up between her shoulder-blades and over the fine white hairs on the nape of her neck. She turned to see the sheep again, huddled close and grazing. She thought about going to church this Sunday. She hadn't been to church since her father died, or was it before her brother's wedding? She thought about going to pray; she'd pray for those in need, pray for the poor. If only she had the power to make them feel better, that would be worthwhile, that would be something, all right. She skipped across the road. On the other side, Roxanne spied one of the furry things that had been squashed. There was no telling what it might have been. She made a face at it, the way she did at most things she didn't understand, or which were out of place, like when a button came loose on her blouse.

* * *

Professor James Moore, day finished, satchel on back, biked home. He was not indifferent to some of the day, the freshly cut grass smell in the air, the sheep in the field, the heat, the little pieces of death that lay here and there along the road. Life was a matter of chance, he concluded. Existing gratuitously, without cause. For James, existence added up to illusions of reason with few worthwhile answers. Perhaps his thoughts were correct, for, as he looked in the field to admire the sheep, his bicycle veered off to the left and the front wheel was struck by a car. To his own amazement, he was not badly injured, only a few scratches, with the wind knocked out of him. But having fallen, his satchel had come undone and his students' papers were scattered helter-skelter all over the road and beyond the fence where the sheep were grazing. The flock stopped eating. Keeping their distance, they began to eye James and the driver of the car, who were clawing, sweating and swearing and straining every facial nerve as they scrambled and fumbled, on all fours, over the rough grounds to gather up the papers. "Hey, here's a snake!" the professor yelled to the driver. And the driver, who was once a poet, said, "A lot of people, like Margaret Atwood, write about snakes these days, write about killing them or keeping them as pets." The professor was angry. "What's that you say?" he asked as he lifted his foot. "That's just the way we are," continued the driver. "We seldom look at the ground. If we do and see a snake, like the one you're kicking the shit out of right now, that's a mystery or a fright. Stupid man, you're frightened by a snake!"

* * *

Harry Lenton, after some twelve years of not taking pictures, took his camera out and walked along the boulevard in the hope of seeing and snapping a picture of one of the tiny creatures before it was squashed on the road. For a bright sunny day, he knew what the light meter ought to read, but he decided to check it anyway and was surprised to see the needle pointing higher than he had expected. He had never used an aperture setting of 16 before. On the brightest day ever, it was always 5.6, never 16. But that was twelve years ago. Why had it changed so much? He swung the camera from its strap. Harry looked up and down the boulevard; except in the field, there were no signs of movement from anywhere else. He stood staring at the road and at the land and at the sheep in the field. He found the brightness, the stillness, very disturbing. Harry Lenton thought no more of taking pictures; he slid the camera into its leather case and hurried home.

POLAR SOIL

Two men and two women came in to do some writing, to compose. They were in long dark days.

They drank tea; the seats were arranged in a semi-circle. The four sat near the fire, so everyone was warm to dream up things to say while watching the flames. There was one man with a red scar across his forehead; he did not sit. He owned the home and stood beside the fireplace. He had a pencil and a piece of yellow paper on the mantle.

"I don't know what to do," the woman with long black hair said. She looked around the room and stroked her hair. "I don't know how we're supposed to start this, this exercise, whatever you want to call it."

"There's no starting to it, just begin," said the man next to her with the hooked nose. He made her think of what Voltaire might look like.

"We think up a line," he went on. "But don't make it closed. We want to be able to keep it flowing, moving along, you see."

"Flowing?"

"Yes."

The other woman asked, "Who's going to start?" She was wearing slim riding boots; she was very young and thin. She had her legs crossed and moved one leg up and down.

"I'll start," the man next to her said. He had a bushy beard. He twisted it and pulled at it, as if it were annoying him.

"Good for you," said the scar-faced man, getting set to write. "Have you got a line?"

"No, I have a word."

"What is it then?" asked the woman with the long black hair.

"The word is . . . the word is . . . *sea*."

"*See*—you say? You mean, to look at?" said the hook-nosed man.

"No, no, s-e-a. As to be by the *sea*."

"Yes, yes," agreed the scar-faced man. "That's a good one. That's a good start."

"*Sea*?" repeated the woman with the slim riding boots.

Everyone smiled at her and watched her leg kick.

The hook-nosed man said, "You have a nice-looking pair of riding boots."

"Thank you." And her cheeks turned pink. "But I don't have a horse."

The scar-faced man who wrote the word down said, "*Sea* is a word poets use. I've read it often."

"So have I," said the woman with the long black hair. She placed a strand of her hair into her mouth.

There was a knock at the door.

"Excuse me." The scar-faced man put down the pencil. "I wonder who it could be?"

Everyone turned to look.

The scar-faced man opened the door. "It's an Indian," he called back to his guests.

"Is he one of our Indians," the bearded man asked, "or is he from somewhere else?"

They waited and listened to the fire. The scar-faced man called, "He doesn't know what kind of Indian he is. He says he's been out looking for a dog."

"I want to see this," said the woman with the long black

hair. She had sucked on her hair so much that the ends were wet. At the door, she quickly studied the man and stated: "He's not an Indian at all, he's an Eskimo. You can tell by the eyes, the round face. Yes, you're an Eskimo."

"Good, I thank you," replied the man. "I am happy to know who I am. I am happy to meet you too."

"I suppose you're looking for some tobacco," said the scar-faced man.

The man nodded.

"That's too bad because we don't have tobacco. You'll have to go further out. A lot further than this place."

"Maybe I'll do that," said the Eskimo. "You haven't seen a dog? You don't have a dog to give me?"

"No, there's no dog here," the scar-faced man told him. "I have to shut the door now, it's getting cold."

The scar-faced man shut the door, and he and the woman with the long black hair returned to join the others.

"Let's continue our writing," the scar-faced man said to everyone in the room. "What was the word?"

"*Sea!*" everyone answered.

The scar-faced man took his position beside the fireplace.

"Yes, *sea*," he said. "I've written it down here. Any other ideas?"

"I saw a fly in here."

Everyone looked at the hook-nosed man.

"That's an interesting line," the young woman with the riding boots said to him.

"No, I mean, it's true," the man answered. "I saw a fly fly by."

"How do you know it was a fly?" said the bearded man. "There shouldn't be a fly around this time of year. Maybe it was an ash from the fireplace."

"Does anyone want to look for it?" asked the young woman with the riding boots.

"Hmmmm, I will," volunteered the hook-nosed man.

"Good, good, let's go then." She stood ready to go.

The bearded man said, "What about what we're doing? Don't you want to continue?"

"Yes," said the scar-faced man. "Never mind the fly."

"Do you want us to give you something to write down before we go look for the fly?" asked the hook-nosed man.

"That's fair," said the woman with the long black hair. "Go ahead, think of something, then try to catch the fly. Bring it back here so we can all see what kind it is."

"You'll have to say something that goes with *sea*," the bearded man insisted.

The hook-nosed man put his head down and rubbed his chin. "Let's see . . . why don't we take the word *sea* and put it in a sentence something like, *the sea was . . . the sea was . . . the sea was—*"

"The sea was what?" cried the girl with the riding boots. "Hurry up and think of something."

"*The sea was . . . the sea was . . . green*. How's that?"

"Yes, that's all right, that's a wonderful sentence," said the woman with the long black hair. "We can use it. Write it down." And the scar-faced man wrote it down, then he read it aloud. "The sea is green," he said proudly.

"No, no," moaned the bearded man. "The sea *was* green."

"Very well, very well, the sea was green," the scar-faced man said. Then the hook-nosed man and the woman wearing riding boots wandered off to look for the fly.

The woman with the long black hair voiced her concern. "We better decide now. Are we going to write a story or a poem?"

"It sounds like it's going to be a story," said the scar-faced man.

The bearded man stroked his beard. "I'd rather compose a poem. That's why I said only the one word when I had my chance. I might have said a sentence with the word *sea* in it.

I might have said a whole line if I wanted to. But I thought we were going to write a poem—now it's a story."

"I think he's right," the woman with the long black hair sided. "Let's change it back. Let's make it a poem."

"Very well," agreed the scar-faced man. "I'll scratch the line out. We'll just have the one word then, *sea*."

"Yes, *sea*."

The bearded man said "sea" too.

"It sounds right," said the scar-faced man.

Suddenly everyone heard the young woman who wore riding boots say, "Yes, yes. That's it! That's it! Oh, I love your nose!" But nobody knew what she meant.

"Have you found it?" called the scar-faced man.

"No, I'm sorry, we haven't," answered the hook-nosed man, "but we've found something else. I think it's a souvenir from the great, great plains."

"Bring it here," ordered the scar-faced man.

The couple came in.

"That's not a souvenir," the scar-faced man said as he pulled the flat object out of the man's hand. "That's a picture of my wife and me. It was taken before we came to this awful place. That's the sky in the background. The whole thing's useless." And he flung it into the fire.

"You know, I've just realized," continued the scar-faced man, "we haven't introduced ourselves."

"It doesn't matter," bitched the bearded man. "Let's get on with the poem."

The scar-faced man gave him a frightful look. "Very well, the word is *sea*."

"How can it be *sea*?" argued the hook-nosed man. "I said *the sea was green*."

"Yes, but it's been changed," explained the woman with the long black hair. "We've decided on a poem now. Saying *the sea was green* sounds too much like a story."

"So it's a poem now," said the hook-nosed man. "*Damn!*

I'm getting sick and hungry too. We came here in good faith and you never offered us anything to eat. Not one bite. How are we supposed to think? How are we supposed to write? Where are your manners?"

The scar-faced man's face turned white. "What do you mean? You had some tea."

"Ha, one drink, so what?" spat the woman with the long black hair.

"I'm sorry, it's been a bad year."

"What do you mean, a bad year?" cried the bearded man. "Every year is a bad year, we all know that, but we still have to have food!"

"Don't do this to us," the young woman with the riding boots said to the scar-faced man. And everyone watched as she lowered her head fast against her flat hands and began to sob.

"Why do you think we came?" said the hook-nosed man. "Can't you see how weak we are? Our stomachs are like little empty cups. Look, like this!" And to show what he meant, he held up a white-knuckled fist.

"C'mon," said the bearded man. "I think we ought to leave. This dim light hurts my eyes and I'm afraid of losing myself and something terrible happening."

"But if you try the poem," pleaded the scar-faced man. "Keep writing and you won't think about eating."

"Of course we will," said the woman with the long black hair. "Food is always on our minds. Lucky for you, we're civilized people. If we weren't civilized, we'd probably just help ourselves to whatever you've got hidden away."

"All right, all right, if that's the way you feel," mumbled the scar-faced man, "go ahead and leave." He crumpled the piece of yellow paper with the word *sea* on it and threw it into the fire. It smoked, then shot up in flame. The four of them stood. Trance-like, they watched it burn.

Outside, as they moved across the wind-swept land, each

one going his separate way, the scar-faced man called after them. "Come again!" he yelled. "The next time you come, I might have some cake to go with the tea!"

But the wind was blowing so hard and whistling so loud that nobody heard what he said. Or, if someone did, there was no indication that he wanted to stop or was about to answer.

LUNAR LANDING

He was too lazy to adjust the strap inside the rim of the hat, so the hat remained loose on his head. It was a white plastic hard hat with a light attached to the front and an electric cord running down to a power pack clipped onto his belt. Hands in pockets, leaning against a tree, he waited for some of the men to clear away from the back end of the truck where they were each being handed an empty family-size juice tin. The young man shuffled over to get his.

"Fill 'er up," the driver said, handing him one. "Then come back here and get another. Remember, the more tins you fill, the more money you'll make."

"Yeah," said a man who was wearing a heavy green shirt with the pocket missing. "And if I don't quit drinking, I'll never quit drinking."

"Right," agreed another picker, who had not put his hat on yet, but who was flicking the light on and off and blinking in a silly way at every flash he gave himself. "And if you don't buy a ticket, you'll never be a winner."

"Wise guys. All I've got here with me tonight is wise guys."

"And if you keep on doing what you're doing, you're going to keep on getting what you're getting," said a man who was short and moved from one foot to the other as if he were trying to keep himself warm. But the air wasn't cold—it was humid. Everybody was laughing.

"Shut up, damn you!" the driver yelled. "Get moving and do what you came here for!" He was a big man with a lumpy bald head so nobody argued. The pickers eased away and walked onto the grounds to find a spot.

The young man, who was only fifteen, found out that there was a trick to grabbing a fat juicy nightcrawler and easing it out of its hole without having it slip through his fingers. Whenever there was a heavy rain, as there was that day, the worms would lie half out of their holes to keep from drowning. One old man, who the kid thought knelt too close and whispered for no reason, showed him the technique: "See, you reach down and grab a crawler," he said, and while he spoke, he was doing it. "Hang on for a second, wait for the worm to relax, then just before he tries to pull away from you, you pull before he slips out of your fingers. See? Out he comes. Easy as pie. As easy as pulling out of a wet whore. It's timing, son. That's all it is, perfect timing."

He could have sworn the man's lips touched his ear.

Picking worms was harder than the boy had expected. He missed at least four before he got one freed and that one looked dead anyway. It was the kid's first job and his first time out. They had been picked up by truck and driven to a park on the outskirts of the city. It was a new park with only a couple of paths and no light anywhere. A few of the tall steel lampposts were standing without bulbs and more lay on the ground. But the city lights were visible along the horizon, twinkling: white, yellow, blue and green.

Counting himself and the driver (the driver had a woman with him; she had sat in the front seat), there were about a dozen people in the park. The area looked as dead as the treetops that became visible whenever the moon poked itself out from behind a cloud. The moonlight made the leafless trees look like giant witches' brooms.

The boy was ready to quit. An hour had gone by and he had only about twenty worms. The driver had said nobody would get any money unless his can was full. The kid now realized it would take him all night to fill his up and, if he did, that would hardly give him enough money to buy a pack of smokes.

Watching the lights, he could see some of the men were already heading back to the truck to cash in their crop and take another tin. He noticed too a large tree that had been chainsawed off near the ground. A tall oak stood beside the stump and so he sat on the smooth cut and leaned his back against the rough bark. He switched his hat light off and lit a cigarette. The stump felt damp underneath him but he didn't care; he was feeling too low about being where he was and doing what he was doing.

Each person had found himself his own particular picking area, away from the others, but then the kid noticed that some of the lights started to move in closer to one another. He had his own light off and took pleasure in knowing that nobody could see him; he purposely cupped his smoke to hide the glow. There were three lights nearing him and it wasn't long before he heard voices and soon could understand what was being said. It amused him to be listening in on a conversation so close to people he didn't know and couldn't see. With the hard-hat lights bobbing up and down, making long shadows on the grass, he pretended he was watching and listening to the sounds of spirits or aliens. But the words he heard were clear and very human.

"There's a guy on his third can already—I saw him."

"Yeah?"

"Yeah, the driver was all smiles, patting him on the back and everything. Heard him say he never seen anyone pick worms so fast before. Even took the guy over to his truck and gave him a drink of something."

"No."

"Yeah."

"Bastard, I betcha he got a good shot of whisky."

"One thing I ain't never done and that was suck up to any bosses. Never kissed ass. I don't care how good I was at doing something—I never kissed ass."

"I bet he drives him right home. I bet he drops him off right at his fuckin' door."

"Well, screw him. I sure as hell ain't coming back out here tomorrow night. You guys?"

"Not me."

"Me neither."

"It ain't worth it. You can't make money picking."

"Look at the size of this one—Jesus!"

"That's a big whopper, all right."

"He's probably full of worms."

"Ha, ha, yeah. A worm full of worms."

"In ya go, you fat juicy mother—fill my can."

"I don't know what to make of that driver. What's he want to go and bring a woman out here for anyway?"

"He doesn't trust her, that's why. I don't like that kind, do you? So afraid somebody's going to take a sniff at their woman."

"Think she's his wife?"

"How the hell do I know?"

"You see the shorts she had on?"

"Where do you think she went off to anyway? Think she's sitting in that truck?"

"Could be in there drinking."

"Maybe. Maybe she's doin' a whole lot more than drinking. Maybe—"

Then, like a bullet through the night, a jet screamed overhead. It had gone so fast that the boy was sure it was a fighter. How much does it cost to house a man in the sky? he wondered.

Now the moon was out and he got to thinking about the astronauts on the moon and how, on the Sea of Tranquillity, they picked up old stones and probably got a pile of money for doing it. And here *he* was, picking up things that were fresh and alive and not making sweet-bugger-all. He butted his smoke and made a move to get up when suddenly there was a hand on his knee and fingers squeezing, pressing down while some words blew at his ear.

"Bitch of a night, isn't it?"

A quick pulse pumped through the boy's temples. He couldn't see the face but he could feel and smell the hot liquored breath. The hand continued holding. The boy, wild with fear, flung his body at the dark figure. "You get away from me!" He leaped up. He swung at the air. He ran. The voice called after him, "Where ya goin', son? I ain't done nothin' to ya!"

The young man's hard hat fell off; it dangled by the cord and, while he was running, the hat swung and hit at his feet. He unclipped the power pack on his belt to let it all fall away. His eyes were fixed on the horizon, on the purple line where the city lights were dancing dots. His tin can was back at the tree. And the voice called again: "What about your worms here, son? Don't ya want your worms?"

A FOILED CANADIAN BANK JOB

He went in. He looked around and took a place behind a man in line. He thought no more of the moment than what went on in front of him. Eyes were watching money. The clock was at three past three. His eyes held the dial. The second hand ticked on. The gun wobbled in his hand. Who said, "May I help you here?" It made no sense to stand still. "Where there's money, there's life!" She didn't understand. "Pardon me?" He cleared his throat. He tried it again: "Your money or your life!" Blue eyes turned white. The whites rolled. Hands hailed the ceiling. A mouth showed. Four screamed. Five ran. Two fell. One became ill. Something hit. A red-tiled floor met his face. The lights he couldn't see went out. A fast song banged, "Silly fool," deep inside his left ear, over and over banged, "Silly fool!" Two pulled his arms. One kicked his groin. His nose bled. Clotted. Caked. It was over. He was glad it was over. On a stretcher, moving across the sidewalk, he smiled for the CBC.

A GOOD BOWL OF SOUP

"The soup's good today," the old fellow said, his spoon a silver blur. "Nice 'n' thick, that's the way I like it." Looking up from his own bowl, the young man watched as the old-timer shovelled in another mouthful of the hot soup. Lizardlike, the man's tongue caught some of the drip seeping down his white-bristled chin. "Times are hard," the old fellow continued, wiping the bowl with a last bit of bread. "Call me a bum if you like, but somehow I feel a lot worse off if the soup's no good, watery—know what I mean?" His eyes rolled wild, then stared down at the bowl again. "Finished," he said. "Good to the last drop!" He pushed the bowl towards the middle of the table, as if now disgusted by it. "How long you been out of work?"

"Too long," the young man said, unwilling to start a conversation. He wanted only to eat and get out. Even if he didn't know where he was going when he left.

"You live around here? Haven't seen you in here before."

"No, I'm not from around here," the young man replied. He lifted his spoon. He ate faster.

"Where you from?"

"Winnipeg."

"Winnipeg?" the old man repeated. He seemed puzzled by the name and then said, "I was out there once. I didn't like it though, too fuckin' flat. Is it still that flat?"

"Flat," the young man said. He swallowed some of his soup. "Flat as a pancake."

"You know what you guys should do out there? You guys should build yourselves a mountain, a big mother of a mountain. Get a look at the city. Bet you guys can't even see your goddamn city unless you're in a goddamn plane. Now in Montreal, we got ourselves a mountain right smack in the middle. Climb up Mount Royal and you get a view of the whole city. You've got to be able to do that, you've got to be able to get up somewheres and look around, get some perspective on life, know what I mean? *Perspective?*"

"I think so," the young man said, but he wasn't sure and didn't care one way or the other. "It's relative," he replied. "It's all relative." He wasn't sure what that meant either, but said it anyway, said it with authority. God knows he'd heard the tone often enough to mimic it. He decided to glare at the old man too, hoping to shut him up. He needed his strength to concentrate on what he was eating. It was an effort to lift the spoon, to open his mouth, to chew, to swallow. It was an effort to stay alive. It would be easier to find a place to jump from. Maybe from that mountain the fellow spoke of.

"You're supposed to take the bowl back!" the old boy said and picked up his own. He gripped it tightly and stared down at the bottom of the bowl with a look on his face as if he now wondered where the food had gone. "Don't expect to get a job in Montreal," he suddenly snapped. "The city's jam-packed with guys like you and me lookin' for work. And you know who's got all the good jobs around here, don't you? Not us. For us, the good jobs are gone. Kaput! Ah, there used to be a time, used to be a time, but not anymore. . . ." His voice trailed off like a record near its end.

Watching him go, the young man believed that the old boy

was right about one thing. The soup *was* good. If the soup had been cold or weak or had had a bad taste, that would have made the day so much harder to face, that would have been one helluva tough thing to accept with so much going wrong, with his stomach hurting the way it was, and the mind bugging his body to bust out at something or at someone who was making up the rules, dealing his cards and playing his hand. The soup. Ah yes, lucky the soup was good today.

WHEN TOMMY TRIP RAN AWAY FROM HOME

Tommy Trip told Billy Right that he planned on running away from home. "Want to come with me?" Tommy asked Billy.

"Why not?" Billy said. "I'm just as fed up with my parents as you are."

"Good, we'll do it together then. We'll take off tonight. I'll stay awake 'til one or two in the morning, then I'll get dressed and come over to your place. I'll jump over the fence and knock on your bedroom window. Be ready, see. Have everything you need to take with you all set to go. But think light."

"That's it? That's the plan?" Billy asked with a look of disbelief.

"Sure is," Tommy said. "No fuss, no bother. We'll spend the night down at the railroad tracks. We'll look for a boxcar to box us all the way to who knows where? Shake on it," Tommy said; he extended his arm.

Early that morning Tommy Trip sneaked out of the house with a change of clothes in a small army-type bag strapped over one shoulder. It wasn't long before he was in Billy's back yard. He went over to the house and tapped on his friend's bedroom window. Billy appeared, rubbing his eyes. He looked out the window with a look that said, *I must be dreaming.* Then he put a hand over his mouth to stop himself from laughing out loud. Tommy motioned for him to come, but Billy shook his head, meaning no—he wasn't going to go after all. And then he put a finger near his ear, made fast circles, around and around, then pointed the same finger at Tommy to indicate that his friend was crazy. Tommy was furious. He made a face back at Billy. Then he realized that if he was going to run away from home, he'd have to go all alone. That would be scary. Imagine running away from home all by yourself.

A short time later, Tommy was home, knocking on the front door. When he had left, he had locked the door. Now there were lights coming on. Now he heard voices. "I don't know who it is," he heard his father say. "But whoever it is, they better have a *real* good explanation for coming around here at this early hour."

TOMMY TRIP AND THE TELESCOPE

Tommy Trip's birthday present was a telescope. The telescope came with a three-legged stand. He set it up in front of his bedroom window. He began to look at distant worlds. He saw the craters and the mountains on the moon; he saw the rings around the planet Saturn and the dark canals on the planet Mars. He saw all these wonders and others too. He saw a woman in a window. She wore a black dress. She had thin arms and thin fingers that pulled a zipper down. The dress fell away from her shoulders, then all the way down to her feet. Gracefully she stepped out of it. She set her hands on her hips and admired herself in a full-length mirror. She was wearing a bright red slip. She fingered a pin from her hair. She shook her head. Brown hair sprang free and fell over her shoulders and then reached the small of her back. She was the most beautiful woman Tommy had ever seen. She looks so close, he thought. It's like I can reach out and touch her.

Through the telescope, through the mirror, he saw a man behind her. He wore no clothes and lay on a big brass bed with a pillow tucked behind him. He was holding something stiff in his right hand and Tommy soon realized it was *that* special part of the man's body.

The woman walked over to the side of the bed and stood in front of the man with her back towards Tommy. She stood there for a moment, as if she might be talking to the man, then she fingered the delicate straps away from her shoulders. She allowed the bright red slip to fall to her knees and then stood naked.

Tommy found it hard to breathe. His right eye started watering. He reached inside his colour-printed race-car pyjamas and took out what his parents had told him was his "little person." Tommy became so involved in what he was seeing and doing that he failed to hear the bedroom door open. The light came on and his mother cried: "Tommy . . . Tommy! My, my . . . what on earth are you doing? Shame on you! Shame! Shame! Shame! What a terrible boy you are!"

Tommy Trip's heart jumped like a spring. He threw himself straight into bed. He lifted the covers up, turned, then buried his head in the pillow. He didn't know what to do with himself.

Tommy's father came into the room. His father took the telescope away. Tommy never saw the new instrument again. He wasn't going to ask about it either. His parents never said a word to him about what he had been watching and what he had been doing to himself. Tommy started thinking that it might have been a dream, that maybe he hadn't had a birthday after all, that maybe there was no telescope, no beautiful lady in a window, no "little person" growing big and getting set to sneeze. This is a very strange world I live in, Tommy thought.

One day, after school, Tommy believed he saw the lady he had spied on. She was standing at a bus stop. Tommy rolled up one of his school scribblers and looked at the woman through one end of the long tube. Seeing the beautiful lady this way, Tommy Trip felt happy and excited inside; he wondered if this was what big people called love.

WHAT THEY DID TO TOMMY TRIP'S DOG

(George's story)

This year, more than anything, Tommy Trip wanted a dog for his birthday and when his birthday came, that's what he got. It was a cuddly little thing and lots of fun and Tommy Trip loved that dog more than anything else in the whole wide world. He named the dog Ranger.

One day, Tommy Trip couldn't find Ranger. He looked every imaginable place he thought Ranger might be: under the bed, in all the rooms of the house, even in the laundry basket, but Ranger was nowhere to be found. I know what I'll do, Tommy Trip thought. I'll ask my brother Bob. Bob was three years older than Tommy; he knew where everything was.

"Hey Bob! Did you see my dog?" Tommy Trip called out, running towards his brother. Bob was playing baseball in a field across the street. "Ranger's over there!" Bob called back, stretching out his arm to point out the distance.

Tommy Trip ran as fast as he could. "Ranger!" he called, "Ranger! C'mon, boy!"

Tommy ran right to where he thought his brother had pointed. He ran with his arms held wide open, so Ranger might jump into them the way he liked to do. But when Tommy saw his dog, he dropped down to his knees and started to cry. The little pup had been hit by a car and was very, very dead.

"Hey, get off my dog!" Tommy screamed to a boy who had his big boot on top of Ranger's little body. Wasn't it bad enough that Ranger was dead? This guy didn't need to step on him too. "Get off! Get off! You big lug!" Tommy Trip screamed as he tried to lift the boy's heavy leg.

"Hey, stop that!" the boy yelled down at Tommy. "I'll be out if I'm off! Don't you know this dog's third base?"

WHEN IT'S ONLY BUGS AND STONES

Something had tickled him. Light as a feather, but nevertheless something had tickled him, there on his thigh, alive, minute. He tossed the covers back. It scurried. A bug. Not large. Not much bigger than a flea, but there it was in bed with him, a horrible thing to find so early in the morning, anytime, especially for Clyde Kleanerson, who had a phobia about being near insects. "Bastard!" he yelled, making a stab at it but missing. It ran full tilt down his hairy old leg. On his second try, he squashed it, flattened it with his thumb, smeared it into fine formless bits. "Nice how-do-you-do," he mumbled, brushing the remains from one hand into the wastepaper basket. "Good God," Clyde moaned. "What kind of room is this anyway? Could that have been a bedbug? A dirty bedbug!" he shouted. And in his sudden anger, he brought his fist down on top of the night table, hard enough to knock over the lamp.

"Is everything all right, Mr. Kleanerson?" his landlady called from the bottom stair. Clyde opened the door. He stuck his head out. "Yes, yes, everything is fine," he said, voice straining. "I just, just stubbed my toe. Nothing to worry about though, Mrs. Shaffer." He waited, listening, hoping she wouldn't ask any more questions. He didn't know why he had said that, lied. Probably because she prided herself in keeping the place so very clean. Well, he thought, if he found another bug, he'd certainly tell her how much cleaner the place could be. Imagine finding bugs in here. What next? A colony of ants? He then decided to take a shower, hoping that it might relax him, and it did.

"And a good morning to you, Mrs. Shaffer," Clyde said, walking into the kitchen. "Did you sleep well?"

"Oh yes, I always do," Mrs. Shaffer replied, patting her white hair with one hand, bringing a cup of black coffee over to the table for this new boarder of hers. "And how about yourself, Mr. Kleanerson, did you sleep well?"

"Yes, fine, thank you," Clyde said, still trying to forget his earlier unpleasantries. After all, this being his first morning at Mrs. Shaffer's home, and the rent being reasonable enough, he thought it best not to make a fuss.

Clyde read the paper and sipped at his coffee. When he had finished, he noticed a stone about the size of a thimble in the bottom of his cup. *How did that get in there?* "Oh Mrs. Shaffer," he called. "Will you come here for a moment please?" He did not look away from the stone. His landlady walked up behind him. "What do you make of this?" Clyde said, lifting the cup to show her.

"It looks like a stone," she said in a matter-of-fact way.

"Of course it is," Clyde said, trying hard not to lose his temper again. "But how did it get in my cup?"

"It must have fallen from the ceiling," she said. "Sometimes that happens."

Clyde, frowning and wondering if he had heard her correctly, looked at the ceiling. What he saw confused him even more. "What the heck is that?" he blurted out. Hundreds of little stones were stuck in the ceiling. They were smooth and round and embedded in a plaster that resembled white sand. "That's not real sand, is it?" Clyde asked.

"Oh no," Mrs. Shaffer said, pouring him another cup of coffee. "It's just made to look that way. You don't think I would be so foolish as to have real sand on my ceiling, do you? The stones are real though. When I look up, I get the feeling I'm underground or living in a cave. How do you feel when you look up, Mr. Kleanerson?"

"I don't know," Clyde said. "It's confusing. I've never seen anything quite like it before."

"Well, I'll glue that stone back in sometime tomorrow. I've too much to do today. It fell out here, see. . . ." She pointed to a spot above the stove. "My good husband made the ceiling. He wanted to do the walls too, but I told him, 'That's enough, I'm the one who has to spend the time cooking in here. If you want to do more of that,' I said to him, 'then do it down the basement.' You see, the poor man was once a miner and he could never get used to living away from it. Why, if he had his way, he would've remodelled the whole house, made it look as if we were living in a mine. Can you imagine such a thing? The man had his troubles, if you know what I mean, but a good man just the same. Did what he could for me." Mrs. Shaffer pulled a kleenex from her apron. She gave her nose a quick wipe. "He died down there," she said. "Right in the basement. Working on whatever stupid thing he was working on. You wouldn't believe the amount of dirt he hauled up out of that place. Said the foundation needed repair, the foundation my foot! I know he was making a tunnel of some sort, building his own mine, poor man. I never went down to see. Except on that day he died, at the foot of the stairs. His heart. Oh, what a strain it must have been for him—what with all of that picking and shovelling, and hardly stopping to eat his meals. I told him to quit, but he wouldn't listen to reason. You know, I'd like to have a look down there myself, Mr. Kleanerson. But I don't like basements." Mrs. Shaffer made some motion to leave the kitchen, then stopped to say, "Would you consider going for me? I would really appreciate having an idea what really went on down there. It's a shame not to know, don't you think?" There was a long pause before Clyde agreed. After all, there was a good possibility that bug he'd found this morning had worked its way up from the basement, and more could be waiting.

"I'll take a look for you, Mrs. Shaffer, but I don't plan on doing a full inspection."

"Oh no, I don't expect you to, just glance around and tell me something about what you see. I'd go myself but with my husband dying right there I'd rather—"

"Of course, I understand," Clyde interrupted, rising from the kitchen table. He took another glance at the hundreds of stones on the ceiling, then asked about the lights in the basement.

"There's a switch up here and another downstairs. Do be careful. The stairs are steep and narrow."

The stairs were steep and narrow. All the way down the wooden steps, Clyde braced himself against the wall. At the bottom he walked into a large cobweb and a big black spider suddenly swung past his nose. Clyde held a hand over his mouth to muffle a scream. He turned and ran upstairs.

"There's bugs down there!" he called out, now holding his hand across his chest. "I saw—I saw a spider in a web. It almost touched me."

Mrs. Shaffer gave Clyde a puzzled look. "You mean to tell me you're afraid of spiders?"

Clyde gasped. "Bugs!" he said. "I can't stand them! In fact, I wasn't going to tell you this, Mrs. Shaffer, but I found one in my room this morning. A very ugly one. Maybe it came from the basement?" Clyde eyed the opening. He walked over and shut the door. He asked for a glass of water, and Mrs. Shaffer brought him one.

Mrs. Shaffer watched Clyde drink his water, then said, "What about if I went down with you? I mean, I don't like being there, but if I'm not alone— I could take a broom and sweep all those cobwebs away for you."

"I don't know." Clyde put the glass down. "Going down there. Is it really all that necessary?"

"No, I suppose not," murmured Mrs. Shaffer. "But I'm so curious. Right now, I can hardly stop myself from wanting to go."

Clyde gave in. "Very well, if you've got the nerve, I must find some too. We'll go together. But you get the broom and lead the way."

They entered the basement. It was between the hot water tank and a small work-bench that Clyde found a narrow opening which appeared to be the mouth of a tunnel. Mrs. Shaffer excused herself to find a flashlight, while Clyde stayed where he was, wishing he hadn't agreed to come. He had never thought of retirement as the time of life to address his phobia for bugs. And not to mention exploring some crazy miner's obsession with digging his own mine or whatever place the opening might lead them into.

"Here we are," Mrs. Shaffer said, flashing the light all over the walls. "Shall we go through the passage?"

"What did your husband do with all the dirt?" Clyde asked, taking the flashlight from her, leaving the broom and showing the way. They had not encountered a single bug; he felt so much more at ease.

"He hauled it all away," she said, "a bag at a time. Some of it he dumped in the yard, some in ditches along the road."

They moved slowly, and whenever Mrs. Shaffer felt a tinge of fear she reached out for Clyde's arm. He rather liked that.

The walls were only as wide as a coffin but high enough not to bump their heads. The air was cold and damp. Everything seemed so deadly still. They spoke in whispers, wondering why anyone would want to spend so much time digging such a seemingly useless passage through the basement wall. Although there had been no real rock to cut through, Mrs.

Shaffer noted again, her husband must have had a tough go of it: picking, shovelling and hauling out tons and tons of the heavy clay-like mixture. At last, when they came to the end, they faced nothing but a wall of earth and a small wooden stool where Mr. Shaffer must have sat to rest when he had tired from digging. Clyde visualized the man looking out towards the light at the entrance, perplexed and pondering why he was doing what he was doing.

"Is this the way it ends?" Mrs. Shaffer said disappointedly.

"Is this the way it ends?" repeated Clyde. "That sounds awfully familiar." He mumbled, "This is the way it ends . . . this is the way the *world* ends . . . this is the way the world ends. . . . Yes, of course, Eliot," Clyde Kleanerson said with a sigh. "Not with a bang—"

"What?" said Mrs. Shaffer. "There's not much for us to see here, is there? Lucky my husband never broke into a sewer line or something."

They returned to the kitchen and had a sandwich and a glass of milk. And under the stony ceiling, while Clyde Kleanerson chewed his sandwich and drank his milk, he pictured a man on a ladder, a man with thick dirty fingers, patiently, one at a time, gluing and thumbing in all the little stones. Clyde was glad to be away from the basement, from the dirt and the chance of running into more bugs. But he also had a feeling of having misplaced something. Or perhaps it was more like after a good meal—waiting for the dessert, only there isn't any.

"It's not like TV or the movies," said Mrs. Shaffer, staring down at her gold wedding band and turning it in circles around her finger.

"What's not like the movies?" Clyde asked.

"The ending," Mrs. Shaffer said. "Usually something happens at the end. We've had a bit of adventure but we've made no real discovery. Just a hole. It was all for nothing."

"Yes, I see what you mean." Clyde realized that her

uneasiness was a lot like his own, but he felt no better for it. In fact, in some strange way, he held himself responsible for Mrs. Shaffer's feelings of disappointment, but couldn't think of anything to do to stop his guilt or to cheer her up.

Sitting in the kitchen, it was easy to hear the clock ticking in the hall. Clyde decided to get out of the house and fill his lungs with fresh air. Mrs. Shaffer suddenly felt very tired and decided to have an afternoon nap.

Outside, the warm air and the bright sunshine seemed to invite him. *Ah yes, how nice.* This felt so much better than being in the house, down in the basement or sitting across from Mrs. Shaffer and watching her sad face. Even the ants scurrying across the sidewalk interested Clyde and warranted little cause for alarm.

LOST ROMANTICS

In the clearing, he saw her hair, then her face, and then remembered. He ran down to her.

"What are you doing here?" he asked.

Not startled, she said, "I'm trying to catch a grasshopper."

"And what will you do with it?" he asked.

"I don't really know," she said. "I might use it for bait and go fishing."

"Fishing with a little girl?" he asked, slowly moving closer. "Like you did ten thousand years ago?"

"Ten thousand years ago?" she questioned with a frown.

"Yes, I met a girl like you, in this very spot, at least that long ago. She had a little girl with her and they were looking for grasshoppers. It was a bright sunny day like this one, and I heard them talking and laughing. I went over to meet them."

"I don't remember anything like that," she said, moving away from him, kicking at the tall grass.

"There's a way to remember," he said. He stepped in closer. His arm touched hers.

"How can I remember?" she asked.

"Kiss me," he whispered.

"Kiss you?"

"Yes, kiss me, and then you'll know. Then you'll know if it was really true."

"I think you're just talking," she said. "Talking and acting silly."

"Then try it," he said. "Just once on the mouth, that's all."

"But you're a stranger," she said. "And I don't go around kissing strangers."

"You only think I'm a stranger. Let me prove to you that I'm not. Let me prove that I'm really your lost love."

"My lost love! You've got a nerve, saying things like that and wanting me to kiss you. I do have a lost love, every girl has one, but you're not him. I'm sure of that."

"Then let me be sure too. Share a kiss with me, so then we'll both know."

He moved so close that she started to lean away, but then, for some reason, she allowed their lips to meet. It was a warm gentle kiss. A magic kiss. Embracing, they heard what sounded like a huge waterfall. This was the sound of ten thousand years spinning into itself.

For a long moment their lips were sealed.

Assured that they had once been lovers, they eased down, deep into the tall grass. Loving and regretting. No, not that they had loved, but regretting that all their days before had passed too soon.

AWAY ON A DIFFERENT BUS SOMEWHERE BESIDES HERE

From the bus window, I see the same old streets: the houses, the fences, the trees, the stores, the poles, the lights, the wires. The objects float by; that is, they seem to move that way, filing through my head, like a counting, like a timing: the sidewalks, the stop signs, the people, the sameness. There's so much of it flowing together, spinning and flapping like the flag-like patches on a multicoloured quilt. What my grandmother makes. Grandmother: she's ninety-seven and likes to be called Nana. She and my mother are very much alike, too much alike. They worry about, of all things, *bowel movements.* Can you imagine? For them, a bowel movement is serious business. If a movement is late, then something's wrong with the system, something needs adjusting. I wish it were only *theirs* they worried about, but they're concerned about mine too. "Did your bowels move today?" one will ask. What a question! As a child, I used to be subjected to inspections. I couldn't flush until they had a good look at what I had done. Sometimes I was praised. Sometimes I was handed a nickel for dropping a good load. Sometimes I purposely ate big meals in the hope of making money. Why would anyone want to check on someone else's stool? Doing that, it's weird. You gotta be demented. Today, in response to the question about going or having gone, I always tell the truth; and if or when I answer in the negative, they tell me to put half a teaspoon of baking soda in a glass of warm water and drink it down. This will clean you out, they say. I did that once, mixed and drank the stuff just to please them, to stop their nagging. In less than five minutes, it felt as if everything between my belly-button and groin had broken loose. I wondered how much of me was going to drain into the bowl. For a time, bent over, holding my stomach with folded arms, I had the shaky fear of losing my liver and kidneys. I was sure I would be in the washroom for a good part of the day, maybe the night too. Going to work was out of the question. I wondered what I would tell my boss. As I sat helpless in the bathroom, listening, one of them did it for me: "No, I'm sorry—yes, that's right, he won't be in today, he's very sick, having a *bowel movement!*" I wanted to die! "Yes, that's right, a *bowel movement*, a big one too. Yes, he's in there now. *Going*." I never went to work that day. I never went back at all. I quit. I won't tell them where I work now. Oh, mothers and grandmothers and *bowel movements*. Is there no other interest in life for them? Why don't they just stay with the darning and the knitting and the quilt-making? Or watch the TV soaps instead of watching me? Speaking of soap. Where are those grandmothers who smell like lavender? What grandmother smells like lavender soap anyway? I hate those kinds of stories. My grandmother doesn't smell like lavender soap. She smells awful. She smells like Sloan's Liniment. And if you get too close to her, she leaves that smell all over you too. Now, with Mother, it's "Chinese Rub." That's what *she* calls it. It's really called QUWAN LOONE OIL and it comes in a little clear bottle with a cork and funny blue Chinese writing strokes all over the white label. On the box, in English, it lists all the ailments it can cure: cuts, burns, bruises, insect bites, sprains, dislocations, fainting fits, stiff muscles, headaches, colds, coughs, stomach-aches, cramps and toothaches. An unexcelled preventive against influenza and contagious diseases. HEALING, REVIVING, SOOTHING, ANTISEPTIC. Then, in small letters, "for external use only." *So, how does it cure the toothache?* Permit no. HU-70695513240. It smells almost as bad as my grandmother's Sloan's Liniment. *Liniment. Chinese Rub.* Bah! I hate them! I want women to smell like Chanel No. 5 or 6 or 7 or 8, or whatever it takes. I want to be able to come out of the washroom and not be asked personal questions. I want to . . . I should be on my own. I ought to be out of the house, away from these women, away from their concerns and their remedies. I ought to be away on a different bus somewhere besides here. I ought to be somewhere out in the country smelling sweet clover, real clover, living in a log cabin, using an outhouse—no flushes counted.

NORTHERN DATES

He sees her waving and stops the car beside the curb. She opens the door and jumps in. They smile shyly. The northern town is small; there is not much entertainment. He is not sure where to take her this time. Last time, they went to a movie.

She pulls down the visor and checks her face in the mirror. She tells him about her parents, that they have phoned and are worried about her living so far away from home. "Daddy still thinks I'm his little girl," she says, smiling to herself. "I've only been gone for three weeks—already they're crying over the phone."

He drives to one of the lakes. They sit in the car, watching the water. She says, "I've never seen so many lakes before—and trees. If someone was lost out here, how would they ever find their way back? Everything looks so much the same."

"Most likely, you'd wait for night," he says. "Watch for the beacon at the airport, then follow it out."

Night comes quickly. There is no moon and the air is cold. He suggests they go for a hamburger, a coffee. She mentions her diet, but says a hamburger sounds good.

The hamburger place is on the other side of town, but that's not very far to drive. On the way, she speaks about being a nurse, how interesting she finds the work, and tells him she gave a man a needle today. "I don't know. I might even go back to school and become a doctor," she says.

They eat in the car. She picks at hers; he gobbles his down and waits. By the time she is finished it is dark. Drinking the last of her coffee, she asks, "What about wild animals: moose, bears, wolves, things like that? Ever see any?"

"Wild animals?" he says. "I can show you wild animals." The idea strikes him as a good one; he knows where to take her now. 'I'll show you *bears*," he says.

"Bears?" she asks. "What bears? Caged? You mean there's a zoo up here?"

"No, no, not a zoo. Bears in a dump. When it gets dark, they come out of the bush to feed."

"*Bears?*" she asks again, as if trying to grasp what this might involve. "What kind of bears, polar bears?"

"No, no, we're not that far north. Just ordinary bears, black bears. Whadaya say? Want to go?"

"I'm not so sure," she says. "Is it safe?"

"Safe? Why wouldn't it be safe?"

He starts the engine. Driving away from the hamburger place, to impress her, he peels the tires.

The road to the dump is full of ruts and ups and downs. If he goes too fast, the shocks let up and the bottom hits hard.

"Damn, that was a big bump," he says. "I'm going to lose my muffler. They should fix this stupid road."

"Where are you taking me?" she asks.

"To the dump. You said you wanted to see the bears, didn't you? Hell, look at that garbage," he says, pulling at the wheel. "Some people are too lazy to take it all the way in."

"How much further?"

"Just over this little hill. Here—" He turns the headlights off.

"What are you doing?"

"I want to sneak up on them."

On the other side of the hill the road opens and disappears

into a large flat space. With no lights on, they see stars and the airport beacon and a bit of brightness showing from town. He drives a little further and parks close to where he thinks all the garbage will be.

"Now," he says, "sit tight for a minute, then we'll turn the lights on and have a look."

"I don't like it here," she says.

"Relax—relax. As long as we stay in the car, there's nothing to worry about."

There is a sound of something moving, tin-like noises.

"What's that?" she asks.

"Hear that?" he says, leaning his chin over the wheel. "That's them. That's bears walking about."

"I want you to take me home," she says. "I don't like this place at all and it smells bad too. Let's go."

"Wait a minute—wait a minute, let me put the lights on, see what we see."

He pulls the switch. There are more bears than he expects. Out of the piles of garbage, at least a dozen heads rise. Red and yellow eyes are blazing at the lights. She gasps.

He says, "Holy Moses! Look at them all: one, two, three, four—"

"I want to go," she says. "Take me home."

"C'mon, c'mon, look at the bears. I bet you've never seen so many bears. Bet there's more bears right here, right in this here dump, than hogs on your daddy's farm. Hey, hey, look at the size of that one! See him there? Right over there. Right beside that stove."

"Please—now! I want to go. Take me home. *Please take me home.*"

He looks at her, then looks back at the bears. Most of them have ignored the light and have started eating again. Two come close to the car. And suddenly he realizes what she's afraid of. It's not only the bears, it's him. She's afraid of me too, he thinks. She's afraid I might do something to her. Say something crazy like: *What's it going to be, honey, me or the bears? Come across or get out!*

"Oh, yeah," he says. "Them bears," he says, shaking his head. "I guess it's not the best place to take a newcomer after all. Especially if one person doesn't know the other one very well. I mean, it's only our second date and all. What do you know about me anyway, not much, right? I mean, I could be a real joker in this here dump, couldn't I?"

He starts the engine, shifts into reverse. She's not saying a word about it. But he notices how she holds herself, arms crossed, fingers rubbing at her elbows.

"Hope I don't back into a *bear*," he says sarcastically.

They drive out along the road in silence. On the way into town, she sits erect, eyes staring straight ahead at the road, lips tight. Even when his anger wanes and he feels some guilt and says he's sorry and then asks if she's okay, there's no response. He doesn't know what else to do but take her home.

In front of where she stays, he stops the car.

"Quite a slough of bears," he says, trying to slough it off, hoping for a chat. "Pretty scary stuff," he continues, "that is, if you're not used to seeing them." She pulls the door handle and pushes hard against the door, harder than necessary. Watching her step out, he says, "See you again? Maybe we can get together on the weekend or something?"

She bends down far enough to see his face and says, "No thank you. Next time, take a trip to the dump yourself. *Idiot!*"

She slams the door so hard the cigarette lighter pops out from its holder. He reaches down to pick it up off the floor. For a moment, he sits there squeezing the cold metal in his hand, then turns it the right way around, slides it into the holder again. Murmuring something nasty about the south, he drives off. There is a funny noise coming from under the car. He knows it's his muffler. "Bloody road," he says, "bloody bears, bloody women, bloody lighter!" He slaps the dash, then quickly catches the lighter as it pops out again.

QUICK DESSERT

What about the ice cream?
The ice cream?
Didn't you say we were going for ice cream?
I did?
Yes, you did.
Large or small?
Large. I want a big one. I want a double-decker sweet cone . . . vanilla.
Sounds good.
It is good.
Go this way.
Which way?
Over here, we can make the light.
Take my hand.
Run!
Oh, stop.
What's wrong?
My shoe's coming off. And I'm out of breath.
Here we are anyway. After you, dear.
What a gentleman.
One ice cream cone, double-decker, vanilla, please.

Sweet cone.

Right, double-decker, vanilla, sweet cone.

You're not having one?

I don't think so. I'll have a chocolate milkshake instead. Why don't you get a seat and I'll bring it over to you?

Okay.

We can sit back there next to the window.

Here you are, sir.

Thank you.

Ah, here we go. Take it, it's dripping.

Mmmmmmmm. Ooooooo, all over my fingers.

Vanilla. Why do you like vanilla?

Mmmmmmmmm, good.

Look at the way you eat that ice cream. You eat it that way on purpose, don't you?

Which way on purpose?

You know what I mean.

No.

Licking it like that.

Like what?

You know.

How else are you supposed to eat an ice cream cone? You gotta lick it, don't you?

Not like that.

Like what?

Running your tongue all over it like it's something else.

What do you mean, something else?

You know.

Oh, as if it were mmmmmmmm. You think I'm pretending that?

Implying.

You're ridiculous.

You're a sexpot.

Oh, is that so? Take a look at this then. Kiss. Kiss. Mmmmmmmmm. Lick. Lick. Gee whiz, I got goo all over my mouth and chin, see? Is it on my nose too? Why don't you lick it off for me?

Here's a napkin, wipe your face. You're grossing me out.

What are you getting so riled up about?

I'm not getting riled up. Look at my milkshake; it isn't thick the way it should be, it's watery.

If it's too watery, take it back.

No, never mind, I can drink it faster this way.

That's it! Suck it up, big boy!

Don't start that again.

Well, you started it. You and your stupid fantasies.

Think I'm crazy?

To some degree, I think everybody's crazy. But you're probably crazier than most. You're the type that might hang around a post office just to watch women lick stamps.

Ho, ho, now who's got the sex-crazed mind?

See, I don't care if I'm silly, you do.

I'm finished. I'm ready to go. I can't eat the rest of this milkshake. It's too cold, and my stomach is beginning to hurt.

Let me rub it for you later.

So when do we have to be back at the office?

We should be there now.

Is there a meeting?

You know, for a vice-president you're a real ass, but I love you anyway.

For an insane president, you do a great job of foolin' people. Your employees really think you know something. But all you care about is dunkin' your tongue in ice cream, sucking up vanilla. And you know what else?

What else?

This place makes lousy milkshakes.

ONE COLD, COLD MORNING

One cold, cold morning, in a bus shelter, stood a body. And because he was standing, not lying flat on the ground the way people who die usually do, the two men who came in walked past him and stood away, off to one corner, away from the wind coming through the open side. Soon, one man noticed how the body leaned, stiff-boarded against the glass, with hands exposed, the fingers white, all too white, all too still, and stiff, with the one hand clutching a computer science book. The man who had been watching turned to the man beside him and whispered, "I think that fellow is dead."

"Dead?" the other man said.

"Frozen."

"Dead?"

"Yes, dead, frozen."

At that moment, an old woman stepped into the shelter. "Excuse me, madam," said the man who had first noticed the body, "but perhaps you should step over here beside us."

"Why?" the old woman asked, shaking. Neither man knew whether she shook from cold or fright.

"We don't want to alarm you, but the person standing there behind you, we think he's dead."

"Oh my Lord! My Lord!" she cried. She turned and saw his open eyes. She threw a hand over her mouth and hurried over to stand between the two men. For a moment, in the watching, there was a long silence, and then she whispered, "Are you sure, really sure he's dead?"

"Quite sure."

"Well, no wonder," she said. "Look at the way he's dressed, crazy fool. Doesn't he know it's the middle of winter? Good heavens, running shoes, and no hat, and no gloves, and on a day like this. Can you imagine? Oh the poor foolish boy!"

"University," one man said.

"What?"

"A university student."

"Yes, look at the book," the other man agreed. "University all right. What do you think of that? What should we do?"

"I don't think we should do anything but wait for the bus. The driver, he'll call the police."

"It's impossible to tell them," the woman said. "You can't tell them anything. They just won't listen to reason."

"Who?"

"The kids today. Think they're so smart. University. That's a joke! I never went far in school, but I always wore a hat and I'm alive today to thank the Lord, and look at him. No, I'm not surprised. University. Ha! All those brains and they don't know what winter is."

The bus arrived. The old woman got on first. She felt the warm air on her face. She couldn't say anything to the driver when he wished her a good morning. She just dropped her ticket into the box and began to sob. The man who stepped in behind her helped her into the nearest seat. She looked around at everyone, then groaned, "Oh his poor mother. His poor, poor mother!"

The last man to get on told the driver about the body. "Are you quite sure, man?" the driver said. The driver was a man from Jamaica. This was his first day on the job. He leaned over the big steering-wheel, widened his eyes and looked past the man standing beside him. He saw the young frozen body. "Eeeeeee man, standing up? Dead. Wow! Believe that, man!" His hands trembled as he picked up the phone. His words flapped out in a wild staccato of broken English. The person on the other end of the line asked the driver to repeat the message. Passengers scraped windows, peered out, talked to each other, talked to themselves.

The police were quick to arrive. Two policemen wearing big warm gloves walked over to the bus shelter. They glanced at the body. Their breath was steaming. They looked at the bus driver and gave him a wave to move on. The driver waited and the passengers were glad he did. They wanted to see the body moved. He was lifted by his elbows and carried like a mannequin to the police car. The computer science book was still in his hand.

A SIGN

Again, Dan Peel had cast too far. Again, he was stuck in the weeds, hooked good this time. And the weather was so hot that Dan's red-lettered GOD IS LOVE T-shirt clung to his back like another layer of skin, absorbing sweat. He would have taken it off, but he had had too much sun already; he was such a fair-skinned young man.

He lifted his fishing rod. He pulled the line some more. He pulled and reeled up the slack until the light aluminum boat glided over to where he was snagged. He could see the bottom. He could see his spinner. It looked like a sheriff's badge shining bright in the tall weeds. With the boat alongside, he gave a couple of jerks on the line and felt the hook come free. He reeled it in; he held the hook in his hand and examined the barbs. They weren't bent. He only had a bit of slimy green to thumb off. He did that and while he readied for another cast, he noticed the shine beneath the surface still flashed from the bottom. Ha, so it wasn't his spinner after all. It was something else. It was something that might be nothing, but he'd soon find out.

He opened his tackle box, reached in and took out one of the biggest hooks he had. It was called a Dare Devil. He clipped it to the leader, then he fed out the line: down, down to the shining object. He began to jig for it and finally the hook took hold. It felt heavy, and with each turn of the reel he feared the object might snap the line. It didn't, but when it neared the surface, damn, if it didn't go and slip itself off, sinking. It dropped in slow motion, moving back and forth, as if it were waving up at Dan all the way, down, down to the bottom. He'd get it, for sure, he'd get it! He'd seen enough of it to know that it was a tin box of some kind. The handle was what he had first noticed shining. He studied the water. It didn't look too deep. He took his clothes off and got in. One try for it and he had it. He broke the surface, red-faced, box in hand. It was an old tackle box, no bigger than his own. With a grunt, he lifted it over the side and set it in the boat. With another grunt, he was in the boat himself. He looked over at the dock and up and down the shoreline. He couldn't see anyone. He didn't expect to see anyone either. Saturdays, the men usually went to town to get drunk. Dan knew he'd be right there with them if he hadn't heard the Reverend Heath's sermon on the radio last summer. Dan used to get drunk and whore around like most of the guys did every weekend. But one particular morning last summer, sitting head in hands (paying the price for the night before), he heard the Reverend Heath say there's a better way with Jesus. The preacher's voice seemed to strike right out to him, right through Dan's very soul. And as soon as the radio show was over, feeling like the lost soul he was, Dan threw up his arms in the pain of his thoughts and gave himself to Jesus. Such a simple gesture. He was saved. *Saved.* He even got himself a pencil and paper and sent away for the free booklet, *What God Wants For You!*, written by the Reverend Heath himself after the man had come out of a deep state of meditation and reflection on what God wanted him to write down for everyone to know. The Reverend was giving his book away for nothing, but he wanted a pledge. It didn't matter how much: five, ten, fifteen, twenty dollars, whatever you could afford or couldn't afford to give, he'd be glad to take it. Dan Peel never sent any money, but they mailed him the book anyway. And since that moment in his life, he hadn't touched liquor or bothered with a woman; he prayed the best he knew how and didn't know why he was feeling the way he was, but he was a man who had his heart opened for some good to come in and he was open for *a sign*. He had one now. He reached down and opened the tin box, which dripped mud and wet all over the aluminum seat. It was a miracle. He had a God-sent sign right there looking up at him: thin and rusted and no bigger than a hunting knife. But there was no doubt in Dan's mind what it was: it was a cross, a steel cross. "I've got it, Lord," his voice quavered. He picked it up. "If you're trying to tell me something, Lord, I'm open for your words." He held the object high above his head. "I know you're giving me something good with this here sign, Lord, and I thank you."

Nobody in the whole world could have made Dan Peel think any different. This was God's doing. It had to be! God made him go fishing today. God directed him to this very spot to catch the cross. God was revealing himself. God was reaching him, giving him more faith than he had known, more than he could hope to find in any Reverend's words. He visualized the cross as a new beginning; he felt that there would be more insights to come and he'd be ready for them when they came. "Show me the way, Lord," he heard himself say. "I'm ready for whatever comes, for whatever you want me to do. I'm ready."

The box was rusted and there was nothing else inside. He slipped it back into the warm weedy water. He thought someone else might happen to find it some day and that there might be another cross inside waiting for them too. Sometimes, that's the way the Lord went about setting things up for people who needed Him. *Glory*, he felt good today. *Glory*.

After docking the boat, he ran full tilt, not stopping until he reached the gate in front of the sawmill. With everyone gone, including the boss and his wife away in town, the place had an unusual stillness about it; it looked dead cold in the afternoon heat. It looked like a lost world with maybe a hundred years between then and now.

Like the other men, Dan Peel had his own makeshift plywood shack, half the length of a boxcar and not much wider. There were eleven shacks positioned all around the sawmill. Except for the black painted numbers above the door, they all looked very much the same: the one door and the one window faced in towards the mill. Although small, they were comfortable enough, with electricity and a cold water tap which you had to leave open in the winter so the water wouldn't freeze. The toilet was outside. Dan placed the cross now on a little shelf above his bunk. Then he lay at the foot of the bed so he could watch the cross and maybe get some hint as to what God might have in mind.

Dan was near sleep when Connie Lear came to the door. She said she had spotted him coming home. She and her husband lived in a huge log cabin which overlooked the mill. Dan wondered what she was doing here and why she wasn't in town with her husband, Frank. Or, for that matter, why she wasn't at home period. It was not right for the boss's wife to be down here socializing with one of the men.

"Mind if I come in?" she asked, moving past the screen door without waiting for an answer. "My, my, but this place is small," she said. "How warm are these shacks in the winter?"

"The winter? They're warm in the winter," Dan Peel said. "As warm as now." He was stunned by her boldness, her fine features. He hadn't been with a woman for a long time—and certainly never one as good-looking as Connie. He now understood why the boss was bent on keeping his wife so close to home: her well-proportioned body looked as if it might, at any minute, bust right out of the thin summer dress she was wearing.

She moved around the room, running her fingertips over

different objects such as the fridge and the stove. Then she walked over beside the bed and smoothed one hand up and down the little wooden table lamp. Leaving it alone, she smiled over at Dan who now stood beside the bed in awe, trying and failing to erase all the old thoughts that had come back to haunt him. Connie made it all too easy to guess what she was wanting. The day, the room, the air, everything was stifling, but here she was making spider legs crawl up and down his spine. It had been a long lonely time. One whole year without the smell or touch of a woman. That's much too long for any man, Dan was thinking.

Connie spied the cross. "And what might this be?" she asked, taking it from the shelf above the bed, turning it over in her smooth hands, tapping the top with her long painted nails.

"I found that today," Dan said, suddenly finding his voice and hearing it strain, and just as suddenly remembering his commitment to the Lord. He went over to her. He took it away from her and put it back on the shelf above the bed. "It's a cross," he said, "an old cross. I found it in the lake. It doesn't mean much."

"Looks like nothing," she said. "Looks like nothing more than some old knife with the end broke off. Can't see how you figure on that being a cross."

"Don't bother about it then," he said. "Maybe it's nothin'. Maybe it's somethin'. Who knows? I just found it, that's all. Found it and brought it home. Stuck it up here to look at."

"All right," Connie said, "don't get excited about it." She flopped herself down on Dan's bunk. She put her pretty head on the pillow and stared up at him. Her dress had risen high above her knees to show off a pair of cream-white thighs. Connie was a redhead and as fair-skinned as Dan. She avoided the sun as much as possible. The little bit of sunshine that she did allow always brought out the freckles on her face. She had a schoolgirlish quality about her. You couldn't tell that she was thirty-three, some seven years older than Dan.

"God, it's *so* hot. Don't you have anything to drink?" she said, kicking off her high-heeled shoes.

"A Coke," Dan said, feeling light-headed, wavy with desire.

"Don't you have any beer?"

"I don't drink," Dan said, heading towards the fridge.

"No, you don't, do you? Now I remember," Connie said. She sat up straight and placed the pillow behind her. "Frank told me all about you, that you're the guy who's got religion. How you don't go to town no more with the boys. Don't bother with women either, I suppose? Just you and the Lord these days, is that it? Just you and Jesus livin' in this here old place?"

"Something like that," Dan said, handing her a Coke and sitting at the end of the bed next to her pretty painted feet. He wanted to touch them. He wanted to touch her all over. He wanted to forget about what he had found, his decision to walk down a new path. You think you got a sign, he thought, then you don't know what you got. You think you got a sign and then you don't know anything about what you thought it was. Maybe she's right, it could be just an old rusty knife after all. He held his breath, hoping to think of a way out, one last chance for some new reasoning to come in and put an end to his wanting her, but it didn't happen. Even the idea that she was married to his boss couldn't dispel and replace what was driving him mad. Right now, nothing mattered more than her being where she was and his wanting her. Watching her mouth that Coke was enough to make him want to cry.

"My, my, Connie. You got a way about you. You really do. You're a real caution." He heard himself say that and couldn't believe he had. With a sweep of his finger, he wiped away the tiny beads of sweat that had formed just above his thin upper lip.

"You goin' to do somethin' good and evil to me today?" she asked, laughing at her own words and setting the Coke bottle on the table. She lifted her legs and picked up the edge of her dress and waved the material up and down like a big wide fan. Dan saw everything. And the strength he imagined he had left was gone too.

In the hot silent room, he reached out for her. She returned his touch with a moan and pulled him down into her warmth. Soon they were sliding wet and naked. The world grew hotter and more wild by the minute. The bed began to rock against the thin plywood wall. The cross fell: from the shelf, to the bed, to the floor. They both heard it fall. They turned their heads to look at the cross and said nothing.

PORCUPINES

It was a hot day with a hot wind. It was so hot we didn't want to move. Although a breeze was blowing, we were stuck in this heat wave.

This was our first outing in the woods for any length of time, a whole two days. And we felt too beat from the heat to do anything but lay around—laid flat out on our unzipped sleeping bags, shooting the bull while we gazed at the clouds. Like I said, it was hot. But this breeze was blowing.

My feet were burning too, so I sat up to remove my boots and socks. That's when I saw the porcupine. He was a big old boy and moved as if he were dead from the heat too. I've seen porcupines in zoos, but never in the wild. A funny feeling came over me about not having anything between us but air. My friend Richard got all excited and wanted to know what to do. I said, "Don't do anything, just keep quiet and see what *he* does."

I'm not sure if the porcupine knew where we were. I can't remember if he looked our way. Maybe he was too hot to care. Anyway, he wobbled straight towards this tall poplar tree. At the trunk, he got on his hind legs, set his front claws into the bark and started climbing. The poplar tree was so smooth, I couldn't figure out how he was going to hang on, but he did. It took him a long time, maybe fifteen minutes to get up near the top, then he changed direction and pulled himself out onto a limb. He looked so heavy on that limb and, with the tree swaying the way it was, I thought the whole thing was going to break in two.

"Will ya look at that," my friend said. "We're down here hot and sticky, and he's up there having the time of his life. Look at him swing!" And that's what he was doing, all right. He was halfway out on that limb, legs hanging, balanced on his soft fat belly. Braced like that (maybe he was falling asleep, I don't know), he swung on that branch, making these long lazy swings, back and forth, back and forth, swaying free and easy. I told Richard I bet he knew all along where he was going, had his mind set on what he was wanting to do. "*Foresight.* That's what these animals got," I said.

* * *

The fall of that year, I was out in the woods again. I was with a couple of guys who, like myself, were following another guy around by the name of Larry. Larry was older than any of us and owned a rifle. He was always looking for something to shoot at. We made so much noise going through the bush, I doubted that we would see anything. But we did. We spotted a porcupine. The animal was climbing up a tall tree and Larry started shooting. The more Larry kept firing, the more the animal's climb slowed. Each time Larry shot, he swore. He shot the rifle until the gun clicked empty. The animal wasn't moving anymore. Larry reloaded, swore, and shot a few more times. Then the porcupine fell. When we got to him, he was on his back and growling. But I didn't think he was growling at us. I thought he was growling at all the bullets Larry had put into him, the hurt he must have been feeling.

Larry shot real close this time. He didn't even have to aim; he just pointed the end of the rifle barrel down at the porcupine's chest and fired. "Buggers are hard to kill," he said. But, as soon as he said that, the porcupine died.

I went home. I wasn't feeling too good. I told my grandfather what had happened. My grandfather said we shouldn't kill porcupines. He said with porcupines around, if someone gets lost in the woods then they've got an animal to eat. He said porcupines move so slow it would be easy to club one if you ever needed to.

I told him I've never heard of anyone doing that. I told him all I ever knew about porcupines was, if they get feeling too hot, they'll climb up a big old tall poplar tree and hang out on a limb and swing, swing in the breeze, and if you watch them do that, that makes you feel happy too. "It's true," I said. "I've seen it happen."

I don't remember Grandfather adding anything more to what I had to say about porcupines. If I remember right, he just fired up his favourite pipe, the one with the long stem, and kept on rocking back and forth real gentle-like on that home-made rocker of his, while I was sitting beside him listening to the runners "creak, creak, creak" on the hardwood floor.

HOME FRONT

It is late. It is raining. A boy hears a knock at a door. Who can it be at this hour? he wonders, rising. He turns the TV off. He waits. He listens. He hopes they will grow impatient and leave. The knock comes again, louder this time.

The boys slips the chain across; he eases the door open and peeks out. Two bloodshot eyes peer in at him. The eyes belong to a man with the coarse beginnings of a grey-black beard. The hair on his head is thin, soaked, flattened by the rain. Between wet strands of slicked-down hair, the scalp, in the yellow porch light, looks like the belly of a fish. He's a short man. And, the boy realizes, a drunk man. He is wearing a long black coat, a coat that looks too heavy and too wet to give comfort.

"Does Bill Penner live here?" the man asks in a low rasping voice.

"Who?" the boy answers, not believing his father could know such a man.

"Bill, Bill Penner," the man repeats, his eyes red and rolling.

"Please, wait here," the boy says. He closes, locks the door again. He hurries upstairs; he calls to his parents in bed.

"What is it?" his father asks.

"There's a man downstairs," the boy says. "He wants to talk to you. I think he's a bum."

"Come in," the father says.

The boy enters and stands in front of the door; he feels and smells the room. The window is closed. He does not like the smell. He wishes to be back outside, standing on the other side of the door.

"A bum?" his mother says, sitting up in bed and rubbing her eyes. "You didn't let him in, did you?"

"No, no, he's down in the porch."

"What's his name?" the father asks. He tosses the covers away, climbs out, puts his slippers on.

"I don't know," the boy says.

"You should've asked him his name." The father moans. He struggles with his dressing-gown.

The boy and the father begin to leave the room. The mother warns, "Be careful, Bill. If you don't know that man, for heaven sakes, don't let him in."

"Don't worry," the father says.

Downstairs, without a moment's hesitation, the father flips the chain off, turns the lock, and opens the door.

There is a long silence. The father looks the man up and down. He says, "What can we do for you?"

The man, with his hands deep inside his coat pockets, sways, squints his watery red eyes, then says in his rasping voice, "Bill . . . are you Bill Penner?"

"Who wants to know?" the father asks.

"The name is John . . . John Speers. I was—"

"John?" the father says. "*John Speers?* Good heavens, man! Is it really you? Come in, you crazy old goat! Come in and get warm!"

The father takes the man's coat and hangs it near a register. He turns to the boy and tells him to make a pot of tea. The two men walk into the living room and the father says, "My God, John, what have you been doing with yourself? You look terrible."

The boy fills the kettle from the hot water tap. The water boils fast. The tea is soon made.

"That was quick," the father says as the boy returns.

The father pulls a short-legged table close to himself and John. They sit beside each other on a wide sofa.

The boy puts the silver tray down.

"One lump or two, John?" the father asks.

The boy sits in an armchair; his feet are flat on the floor. He breathes very slowly and sits very still.

"Two, please," John says, coughing once, leaning forward, resting his arms on his skinny legs. He watches every move as if he has never seen tea poured before. When cream and sugar are added, John lifts his cup with both hands. He trembles, makes rude noises while he drinks, but does not spill a drop.

"You make a fine cup of tea," he says to the boy.

The boy smiles shyly.

"He's your boy?"

"Yes, that's him all right," the father says. "He's the only one we have."

"I was married once," John Speers says. "I've got a picture here, somewhere." He begins to search. He is wearing grey dress pants; they have a high-gloss greasy shine. He reaches around to the back pocket and pulls out a well-worn wallet. He begins to finger through all the hidden compartments.

"Nope, can't find it now," John says. "We had two girls, twins." He closes the wallet and stuffs it into his pocket again. Now, fluttering fingers race through a horribly wrinkled sports jacket. The jacket is too large; the sleeves hide half his hands. Two buttons are missing, and the remaining one hangs by a single thread.

The father says, "It's all right, John, if you can't find the picture, it's okay." But the man acts as if he doesn't hear anything. He pulls out pieces of paper from one pocket, a comb from the other, then, from the inside of the jacket, a razor and a toothbrush. Poor, poor man, the boy thinks. All he owns is with him.

"John and I were in the war together," the father blurts out. The boy is surprised. The man stops his search.

"Yes sir, that's right," agrees John. He looks up; he leaves his pockets alone. "What a life that was," he says. "Who can forget it? Remember that day we got pinned down and you had your darn fool head up so high with all those bullets bouncing around us? Crazy, how you never got hit. Remember? Remember, dust got in your eyes?" John shifts on the sofa with excitement. His eyes are wide. "Your father thought he was blind. He was on the ground yelling, 'Help! I'm hit! I'm hit! I'm blind! I'm blind!' But when we got to him, all he had was dust in his eyes. Imagine that! Boy, when we got out of that spot, did we have a good laugh. Remember that?" John shows a wide brown smile. He taps the father's knee. "Remember? Remember?"

"I can't forget it," the father says. He lowers his eyes and wrings his hands. "I thought I was done for. . . ."

The boy had never heard that story before. His father had only talked about the food they had eaten, how bad he had felt going over, how good he felt about coming home, a few funny stories, but never anything like this, being shot at, coming close to being killed. The boy was anxious to hear more of these stories from this John Speers, this ghost-like figure from out of the past.

"Then there are those things that come in at night, Bill," John continues, voice straining. "Horrible things. Monsters. Dead eyes. I lose sleep. I hate my life— There seems to be so much pain in the world, so much pain in me, hurts—scars that won't heal." With a sleeve, John wipes a tear away. "Sorry," he chokes back, "I shouldn't be going on like this—not in front of the boy."

"That was a long time ago, John," the father says. He reaches up and rests his hand on the man's shoulder. "It's best to leave it all alone now. Care for some more tea?"

"No, no thanks," John says, eyeing the boy, who looks down and away. John stands and almost falls. The father catches him in time. He holds the man's arm and waits for him to regain his balance. "If I don't leave now," John says, "they'll be locking me out. You see, I'm in a different army today, one of *salvation*."

The boy gets John's coat. It is still wet. The father goes upstairs. He returns and puts something into the man's hand. John shakes the father's hand vigorously and thanks him over and over again. "Someday I'll get right with myself and pay you back," John says. "You'll see. And you—boy!" He puts his hand on top of the lad's small head. "You make a real fine cup of tea, son. It warmed me; it made me feel good."

From the front window, the boy and the father watch the man steer himself along the street. "You can't do much for a person like that," the father says, continuing to gaze out the window. "You ask a man like that to stay and you only ask for trouble."

The boy says nothing; he thinks he understands what his father is trying to say. He wonders if the craziness inside John Speers is inside his father too. Did he not hear his mother say that his father had terrible dreams, something like "fits"?

The boy had never seen his father drunk, never heard him talk crazy the way John Speers had talked. But what if he did? What would happen then?

"I'm going to bed now," he tells his father. "Good night."

"What? Oh yes," the father says, without turning away from the window. "Good night, son. I'll be up soon too."

THE PLACE

Frank is hearing sounds around the house he's never heard before. The fridge goes on and off. (Too often, he thinks.) The floor-boards, although very new and very thick, creak. The china rattles whenever a heavy truck rumbles by. A neighbour (whom he's never met) starts an engine—she's going to work. Frank's not going anywhere this morning. He's out of work. He sold his businesses. He used to own a restaurant, a book store, and a novelty shop, but before he starts something else, he wants a holiday. What Frank thinks he needs right now is a little more meaning, a little more . . . Well, something different, something not so familiar. He's forty-four, mid-life crisis time. What did the singer Neil Young say? "Better to burn out than to fade away." Frank will take a trip, a Caribbean cruise. It's not the season for it, but what the heck, he feels like going and he's going to go.

* * *

The woman who has left him phones this morning. She tells him she's going to take all the furniture. She's coming for the dishes in the morning. Frank won't be here when she arrives. She won't like that, his not being here, not giving her a chance to make another scene with her daughter watching, like her performance the day she left, the day she said: "Screw you, *asshole!*" First time he had ever heard her swear like that. They were together for four years. The day she left, she screamed, cried and threw things around the house. She even broke one of Frank's CDs. She can have the furniture, he decides. She can have whatever she deems necessary. One thing he won't miss is that friggin' dog of hers. Her leaving, taking him with her, saved the little bugger's life. Imagine, at his own front door, the little fart wants to nip him—but sees the postman and wags his tail. Frank won't miss her snotty little daughter either. She's fourteen now and only thinks about boys and clothes. They hardly speak. Whenever she does say something, it's only because she wants money. Frank can't remember the last time the three of them sat down at the dining-room table, like they do on TV commercials, the family get-together, all around the dining-room table; father cuts into a big fat juicy roast beef. Everybody's happy.

Frank will take what he needs in the car. He'll rent a one-bedroom apartment downtown. He has books, clothes, bedding, towels. Frank takes whatever is on his side of the bathroom cabinet. As far as the bank money goes, he reasons, if she wants half, she can have half. Why be greedy? Besides, being good to her right now might help him avoid a long-drawn-out battle later on. Actually, he's been quite lucky, she's left him with the better car, but that's probably because the gas gauge was showing empty on it. When he returns, he'll put the house up for sale. He hopes they will settle matters out of court. He dreads the thought of having a couple of blood-sucking lawyers draining his account.

* * *

There's nothing much going on, on the boat. Not many people are taking cruises this time of year, early fall. But it's relaxing, watching the water during the day, the black sea above at night, the mysterious star-studded sea that leaves Frank wondering what's so damn important about his place in the universe anyway.

Two days out, the captain lends Frank his binoculars. Good fellow, he thinks. He watches the ships sail by. He notices a lot of oil tankers. And, on deck, he focusses on the women sunning themselves, not very appealing though. Even the young ones look tired, worn out, drained, as if they've been through some kind of ordeal.

The third day out, he's drinking quite a bit. Frank begins to say things and do things he really doesn't mean to do or say. When the captain asks Frank to give back the binoculars, Frank calls the captain an "Indian-giver." The ship's steward strongly suggests that Frank go below, "to sleep it off." Reluctantly, Frank obeys orders.

* * *

Frank gets off the boat and books into the package tour's hotel, a hotel called SOUTH SEAS HOTEL. He has his bags put into his room; he goes to the bar for a drink. After a few too many, he leaves. He begins walking down or up, he can't remember which, up or down, a deserted beach. He hasn't eaten all day. He falls asleep on the sand. He wakes up and walks some more. He ends up at a place called THE PLACE HOTEL. He enters the bar. He orders a sandwich and a beer. He doesn't know why he's drinking so much. Yes, he does know why. Frank was on the wagon for more than a year. The longest dry spell he ever had. Now, when he lifts the glass, he thinks, *Damn it all!* How—why—did I ever get started again?

* * *

It was yesterday when Frank stumbled into The Place Hotel. So, counting the new apartment he has rented back home, the room with his bags, the ship's quarters, and now this spot, that's four different places in two days. But he has no idea what this all means.

* * *

It is morning. A woman is sleeping in Frank's bed. He closes the door and sneaks downstairs. He's trembling. He is in need of something strong—and fast. Here, in the bar, in The Place Hotel, which is like an oasis after that stretch of sand he was on, Frank orders a whisky. He eyes the glass, thumbs the rim, thumbs small circles, then moves a finger up and down the round coolness. He lifts and tilts the glass and knocks 'er back. Now Frank orders a beer. The foamy beer flows like a cool creek on a hot summer's day, a welcome run down his parched throat. He takes another swallow. He sees the bar through the bottom of the glass: egg-shaped. Mysteriously locked inside the glass, the barroom glimmers like a painted picture dish. For some reason he begins to wonder if the first pair of eyeglasses were invented this way—peering through the bottom of a beer glass or bottle—knock two bottoms out and hook them together. *Voilà!* The first pair of eyeglasses. *Oh, the marvels of whisky, cold beer.*

"Another?" the bartender asks, taking the glass. With a sweep of his white towel a wet ring disappears.

"Why not?" Frank says. "Yes, another beer." He can feel his skin beginning to cool. Or, is it numbing? The mirror in front of him covers most of the wall. He squints. *That doesn't look like me.* He studies the bottles that stand in rows below the bottom frame. They remind him of soldiers: tall and ready, straight and narrow, clean and smooth, long-necked, shining, some in white, some in brown uniforms, all flaunting their unified strength. Frank was once a soldier. He hated it. He resented the drills, the discipline, the thoughtless commitment. He was booted out in sixty-six. I was ready to call it quits anyway, he says to himself. If there's going to be mindless commitment, it ought to be to yourself, not to an army or a country, not to a woman or a family, not to your mother or your father, not to anything or anybody. In the end, death or disappointment, that's what commitment gives you.

"Don't particularly like people who make a mess when they kill themselves," the bartender says as he looks at the clock on the wall.

What's he mean by that? Have a lot of people committed suicide here? Guys like me? Is this the dropping-off place— The Place Hotel? Frank looks away from the bottles and the mirror and grins. He shakes his head. "How long have you lived in this place?" he asks.

"The Place. How long? Long time."

"Like it here?"

"Never gave it much thought. Guess one place is as good as the next. The Place," he says and looks more thoughtful.

Frank is almost finished his second beer. "I've never been in this place before," he says. "Strange name, The Place. Is it big enough to be a town? What happened in here last night anyway?" *Perhaps I should not have asked that last question?*

"It's a town and you were here last night. You were here *late* last night." The bartender's bushy eyebrows narrow into a dark V. "You were here and not alone. You had a young black woman with you, a real good-looker. Remember? The two of you sat over in that corner, right under that horse painting." Frank glances over his left shoulder; he studies the horse painting. On the far wall is a huge picture of a white stallion galloping hard across a silver cloud. The head's all wrong: the nose looks disjointed, the eyes are too beady for a horse's eyes; the ears are too small too. He is about to ask the bartender if it's really a horse when suddenly and proudly the man states: "I painted it!"

"Oh, you did," Frank says. "Did you?" He doesn't want to hurt the guy's feelings. "Well, good work . . ."

"Thanks. You were sure drunk when you sat down," the bartender says.

"When—now?"

"No, no, last night. When you were here with your lady friend." He picks up a glass and begins to shine it. "You guys got to laughing so much I thought you wouldn't be able to stop, then you started singing, singing that song: "Hang on Sloopy, hang on—" Finally, I told the waitress not to serve you anymore. You didn't seem to mind. I think you just thought the bar was closing."

"So that's why my throat is so sore," Frank says, fingering his neck. "Singing? Me? Ha! I guess I raised my voice too high."

"Maybe you raised more than that," the bartender says, forcing a belly laugh. Frank looks down and grins shyly at his empty glass. "She's still in my room, sleeping, I think. A real sleeping beauty she is, lovely. I can't remember all that much about her, where we met. Guess she's still in the room though. Boy . . . was I dry this morning. Glad you were open early."

Frank shoves the glass away and orders another beer. He would rather have a whisky, but he knows the beer will take him to where he's headed a lot slower. He doesn't want to pass out this early. *Need to get my bearings. The woman in my room, I don't remember having much to do with her last night. That is, I don't remember sex.*

"Yes sir, glad you were open. I was dry as a desert. Dehydrated real bad. The Place Hotel. How did I ever get to The Place Hotel?" He eyes the mirror again. His hair is uncombed. He needs a shave. *What's so different about me? It looks as if I've been shipwrecked.* "What's The Place all about anyway?"

"You want to know something about The Place?"

"Yeah."

The bartender smiles at his only customer. He leans on the bar. He looks as if he's about to reveal some dark and mysterious secret. Instead he drags the weight of the day with every word. "Not much really to tell about The Place," he says. "It's a little resort by the sea. People come, people go. Not much money in The Place. Not much of anything. Except the beach, nice white sand. I like the beach, living by the sea." He straightens himself. "Why, there's no more than a hundred people living here. That keeps it quiet. There's no school for the kids. I'm glad there's no school for the kids. *Kids.* Nothing but trouble."

"By the sea, The Place is by the sea, you say. Where by the sea?"

"What do you mean, *where by the sea*? By the sea is by the sea. How did you get here anyway? How far did you walk up the beach?"

The question puzzles him. He stammers and drawls, "I . . . I must've walked up the beach—a long ways—I must've walked an *awfully* long way."

"Yeah, well, you wouldn't be the first one to come that way, up the beach, I mean. People get confused. Instead of staying where they are, they walk up the beach. They end up at The Place. Some even miss their boat home. Don't matter though, it's good business for me when they do." He giggles and shakes his head. He ambles down to the end of the bar. From a cardboard box he starts stacking new bottles up on a dark wooden shelf. Frank decides to finish his beer and go up to his room.

* * *

She is naked on the bed. He stands over her and admires her beauty. She stretches her long thin arms up and over her head, then drops them down to her sides, palms up. Her eyelids flutter, then open. She smiles. She looks as if she couldn't be in a better place than where she is. "Glad you're here," she says, blinking sleep away, yawning. "I feel good now, rested. Want to finish what we started last night?" Frank stands beside the bed; she reaches out and diddles her fingers between his legs, then gives his balls a gentle squeeze and smooth-over. Her hand is like a tiny wave, lapping over his wrinkled and soiled pants, teasing him, waking him. He shivers. He's dizzy from the booze, but he's thinking a moment like this, a rare moment like this, ought to be remembered forever. If only the mind could recall a clear picture whenever it wanted to. If we had that ability, psychiatry—psychiatrists—wouldn't exist, we'd never get depressed.

He reaches down and runs his fingertips over her bare breasts, over her oak-coloured acorn-shaped nipples. They rise. He bends over to kiss them. Sucked, they swell. They swell hard. They glisten like wet bark.

"I want to shower," she says, and lets herself slide out. She stands and moves away from him. She is tall. She is bone. *Muscle. Flesh.* She is all things.

As Frank watches her going she stops. She turns and comes to him again. She raises her long dark brown arms and feathers her fingers over and around his neck. She steps in close and kisses him on the nose, on the ear, on the cheek, on the chin, then moves away with a whisper: "I'll only be a minute. I can't wait for us to fuck," she says, sounding the words "to fuck" as casually as one might say "to eat," or "to sleep," or "to be."

In the small washroom, the water is splashing against the pink plastic curtain. Frank steps inside the shower. She looks pleasantly surprised. His bony chest presses hard against her hard skin-tight breasts. She hands him the soap. He rubs to create a frothy white foam, which makes him think of the surf washing over dips and mounds of wet sand. Her mouth teases, full and open. The water runs over her mouth; the warm wetness enhances the unfamiliar yet inviting purple lips. She kisses. Tongues. Their tongues are long and eager. Delightfully, she slips hers in, far in, deep and daring. Then she slides downward, licking at the hairs on his pale wet chest, then lower and lower, until she has him where he wants her to be. "Oh, yes . . . Yes," Frank cries. "*That's it! That's the place!*"

* * *

He likes the way her hair shines in the midday light, the way her tiny black curls lie on the off-white pillow.

"I'm a little confused about it all, you know. I don't remember much. When we met on the beach, did I—"

"We never met on the beach," she says. "I was standing in the lobby. You said, 'Let's go for a drink, sweetheart.' So that's what we did; we went for a drink, and here's where we ended up. Remember?" She turns. She lifts her head and leans on one elbow to see him. "No, you don't remember, do you? Guess you were pretty drunk." She taps the tip of his nose with the tip of her finger.

For a long while, they lay still, listening. On a rusty window screen, a fly buzzes. The smell of their sex is heavy in the room. They sleep; they wake; they sleep some more; they wake; they dress. They leave the hotel room and go down to the beach for a swim.

The whiteness is there, everywhere: white sea, white sand. The sun is like a white-hot stone in a not-so-white sky. Lazy waves wash and cool their bare feet. He holds her. She tells him her name is Sue Ann. He takes her hand and smiles, smiles at what he thinks is a false name and at his own unveiled dead-fish whiteness. In the foreground, he spies a ship sailing. Gulls are flying overhead, squawking.

They swim naked. The water is cold, refreshing. They swim hard. Frank allows the salt water to fill his mouth. The water stings his gums. He can feel Sue Ann beside him. He feels the air, the sun, his own buoyancy. Her arms lock around his neck. They stand in the shallows. She lifts and places herself, long legs locked around his waist. He decides right then and there to try to remain at The Place for as long as possible. For as long as the mornings are close to being as good as this one, he has no wish for anything more familiar.

COUNTRY QUIRKS

Grandma took a loaf of bread out of the oven. Norman Todd and Joy Joy came into the kitchen. Norman Todd asked, "Where's Grandpa, Grandma?"

"Ain't he in the house?" Grandma said. She set the hot pan down onto the sideboard.

"We can't find him nowheres," Joy Joy said. "We even looked in the yard, thought he might be smoking his pipe under that big old shade tree, the way he likes to do, but he's nowhere to be found."

"Well, maybe he went and laid himself down? Did ya look in the bedroom?"

"Yes, ma'am, we looked everywhere. He ain't in the bedroom neither. He ain't no place we looked. We looked all over and we can't find him."

"Don't tell me," Grandma said. "Don't tell me that old man has run off again. He did that once before. We couldn't find him no place. Sunday morning he was gone. Got up and had breakfast and was gone, disappeared. Took us all day before we found out where he was." She cut and gave each of the children a big slice of the warm bread.

"Where was he, Grandma?" asked Norman Todd. He took a knife and put a pat of butter over the warm bread.

"Where was he? He was up in the meadow, that's where he was, smoking his pipe and staring at a pile of old logs. Dreaming about his wood-cutting days. He was all dressed in his Sunday best too. Told your cousin Albert, that's who found him, told Albert that he wasn't going to go to church no more. Said that church was full of people that was lacking something or looking for something he wasn't looking for."

"You think he might be there now, Grandma? You think he's in the meadow now?"

"Well, he might be. After all, it was a Sunday morning the last time he was gone and this is a Sunday morning. You're the only ones here today, so guess I'll have to send you off to look for him. But if you don't see him in the meadow, I'll call Cliff Richards to come with his dogs."

"Don't worry, Grandma. We'll find him," Joy Joy said. She did a little circle dance around the table. She sang, "We're off to find our grandpa, Grandpa John, who's gone, gone, gone. Gone far away—"

"Don't go getting yourselves lost now. Don't go any further than that meadow. If you go beyond the meadow, those woods will eat you up, then we'll have to get the dogs to find you too."

The children followed the old logging road to the meadow. "You see Grandpa's tracks?" Joy Joy asked, trying to keep in step with her brother.

"That might be his tracks," Norman Todd said, pointing at the ground. "It's hard to tell; this road's so old and hard."

"What if we find him and he's dead?" said Joy Joy.

"Don't talk like that!"

"Well, it could be true, you know."

"You're morbid."

"What's morbid?"

"Morbid is when you think— Here! Look at that! A deer!"

"*Where?*"

"There."

A big buck bolted and ran off ahead of them.

"Wow, was that a beauty," Norman Todd said.

"And so close."

"We could've gotten closer, but you screamed."

"No I didn't."

"Yes you did. 'Where?' you said. 'Where?' "

"I did not."

"You did so."

"I just said 'Where' once."

"So that's when he ran off."

At the meadow, the road faded. The only thing higher than the grass was the huge pile of logs Grandma had talked about. "Look for a shady spot," Norman Todd said. "That's most likely where he'll be sitting."

They stepped over the high grasses and began to walk around the meadow. "Is that him sitting there?" Joy Joy said, pointing.

"Hey, I'm sure that's him," Norman Todd said. They both started running. Grandpa was sitting under a big old shady tree and he was smoking his pipe. He was all dressed in his Sunday best too, dressed the way Grandma said, just like the last time he ran off. "Grandpa! Grandpa!" the children cried. They got to him and they threw their arms around his neck. "We found you! We found you!"

Grandpa smiled and said, "You found me all right."

"We saw a deer," Joy Joy said, hugging the old man again. "Grandma said you was lost up here. She said you didn't want to go to church no more."

Grandpa took off his straw hat and wiped his forehead with his sleeve. His face was a putty white.

"You okay, Grandpa?" said Norman Todd. "You're sweating real bad. Even in the shade you're sweating buckets."

"I've been sweating buckets ever since I started walking up that road."

"You don't look too good," Joy Joy said. "You look worn out. You're not going to die are you, Grandpa?"

"I'm worn out. I'm worn out from walking. Worn out from the heat too, worn out from living with your grandma so long, but I ain't planning on dying today."

"Did you cut those logs, Grandpa?"

"Me and your Uncle Roy cut those logs, a long time ago, we cut those logs. They were the last ones cut. Your grandmother wanted an electric stove. I got her one and didn't have to cut wood no more."

"We better be getting on back," said Norman Todd.

Grandpa asked, "What did Grandma say? Did she say anything about my leaving home? Last time, know what she done? She hit me on the head. She made a big bump on my head. I'm too old to be hit on the head. I don't want to be hit on the head no more."

"Hit you on the head?" Joy Joy said. "Why would Grandma want to do that?"

"She hit me with that cast-iron frying pan. She'll do it again too if I don't watch out. I bet she will. You watch. I'm too old to be hit on the head."

"*Naw*," Norman Todd said. "You're making that up, Grandpa. I don't believe Grandma would ever do something mean like that to you, not to you or nobody."

The children took the old man by the arm and helped him up. They walked a few steps, then Grandpa said again, "She did it all right. She hit me square on the head. Knocked me out cold too. Maybe with you kids here, she won't do that, that's what I was thinking this morning."

Joy Joy let go of her grandpa and skipped out in front of him to sing, "Yes, yes, she hit him on the head with a frying pan—"

"Shut up," Norman Todd said. But Joy Joy sang, "Grandma *please, please* don't hit my grandpa on the head no more and make him sore—"

"I told you to shut up," Norman Todd yelled.

"Shut up yourself," Joy Joy said. "We saw a deer, Grandpa, right here, we saw a deer."

"A big buck deer," said Norman Todd. "There's his tracks."

"Must've been a big one all right," said Grandpa. "There's a lot of deer come around the meadow."

When they reached the house, Grandpa looked more worn out than ever. "We found him," said Joy Joy, her little eyes rolling. "He was where you said he was, in the meadow, Grandma."

"I'm going to bed," said Grandpa. "I'm all worn out from the sun and walking up and down the road."

The children stared at the frying pan. The cast-iron pan hung on a nail behind the stove. Grandma never said a word. She was busy at the kitchen sink. She never looked at them, only raised her head to look out the kitchen window.

"I feel like some fried biscuits," said Joy Joy. "Would you make us some fried biscuits, Grandma?"

"What? Fried biscuits? We're going to have dinner pretty soon. You children run off outside and play. I got things to do. I don't want you in my way. I'm glad you found your grandpa though."

"He came home real quick like, Grandma," said Norman Todd. "He didn't give us no trouble at all."

She wiped her hands on her apron. "That's good. That's fine now. You children did real good at finding your grandpa." She came over to them and pressed them on towards the door. "Out you go now."

Joy Joy touched her brother's back and watched her steps. When the door had closed, Joy Joy said, "She's going to hurt Grandpa, I can tell she's going to do something bad to him. What can we do to save Grandpa?" Her brother put his arm around her. "Never mind, Grandma won't be doing nothing to him. She wouldn't want to hurt him none with us around.

She knows we'd tell. Soon as Pa came up for us, we'd tell him, then she'd have to go to jail."

"Maybe she wants to hit us too," Joy Joy said. And then they decided to sneak around the house. They put their ears against the wall, but never heard a sound. At one end of the house, Norman Todd lifted his sister up so she could look through the kitchen window, but she said she couldn't see anything and wanted to be let down right away.

"I guess we can't do nothing but wait," said Norman Todd.

"Why don't we pick some wild flowers?" Joy Joy said. "We'll pick some flowers for Grandma, then she'll be happy, then she won't be thinking about hurting Grandpa."

Along the gravel road, there were lots of wild flowers, and on the way back they heard Grandma calling, "Dinner! Dinner!"

When they went into the house, the first thing Joy Joy noticed was that the frying pan was missing. She dropped her flowers on the floor; she held her hands up over her mouth. Norman Todd ran into the bedroom. Beside the bed, the frying pan was on the floor. Grandpa was propped up, shoulders against a pillow. Norman Todd could see an egg-sized bump on the old man's head.

"What happened to Grandpa?" Norman Todd asked; his blood was running hot and cold.

Joy Joy was too scared to move. All she could do was stand there and wring her little hands, while Grandma began to tell the children how their grandfather had gotten out of bed to get the frying pan, how he was afraid she was going to hit him on the head with it. "Imagine thinking that?" Grandma said. "And here, if he didn't go and hit his own self on the head, tripped over the bedroom rug." She pointed at it. The children squinted. The rug looked wrinkled on the floor. "When he fell he hit his head on the dresser," she said. "Knocked himself out cold, as cold as a cucumber, poor man."

"Gee, Grandma," Joy Joy said. "You sure he's all right?"

"Don't you worry none about your Grandpa John, he's a tough old bird. Why, first thing in the morning, he'll be asking for his breakfast. I don't want you kids to be telling anyone how silly your grandpa is now, you hear me? There's folks around these parts mean enough to put an old man like that away."

Norman Todd looked at Joy Joy. Joy Joy looked at Norman Todd. They didn't know what to do or say. Grandma's eyes were on them. She coaxed the children over to the table. The big pot of stew smelled real good.

"Your Grandpa John don't know what he's missing," she said as she took hold of a large wooden spoon and began to dish out the food. "But that's the way it goes, ain't it? It's all his own doing anyway. Sometimes he makes me so mad. C'mon now, children, eat up."

Wordless, eyes fixed to their plates, the children reached for their spoons. They did not slouch. They kept their elbows off the table. They chewed their food well.

MY MARK ON THE WALL

Virginia Woolf had a mark on the wall. The mark was a snail. This morning there's a mark on my wall, but it isn't a snail. It doesn't look like anything alive. My mark is eye-shaped, eye-sized, and so transparent that the white painted wall is visible behind the colours: green, red, and blue. My mark is a watery rainbow. How it got there, so high up on the wall, so near the ceiling—I can't imagine. But on my bed, hands cupped behind my head, I look at the mark and wonder about things, like my aunt, the way she keeps playing the piano. Even with the door closed, I hear the notes. Not that I mind the piano, the instrument is lovely; it's the same piece over and over again that bothers me. There's other things in life besides *opus three, number two*. For instance, before Father died, my aunt played and sang hymns on Sundays. I know what it is. My father, who was her only brother, was like a father to her. And so it hurts all the more. Who am I to talk though? I haven't been out of the house since the day of the accident, except once, two days ago, I walked in the garden, did some pruning and watered flowers, but then I felt so exhausted I had to have a lie-down. *The flowers.* Maybe seeing the flowers reminded me of the funeral. I had thoughts about the ladder too. I was to hold the ladder steady for him, and that's how the accident happened. I was to hold the ladder steady while Father looked over the roof to see if anything was in need of repair. But I let go. I let go to take a swing at a bee that buzzed my nose. Father fell and died instantly. Ironically, he was down on the ground with the bee now sitting on the tip of his nose. No need for me to stare at my mark on the wall to remember the tragedy. I'm haunted by nightmares. And Auntie plays the piano to stop from going mad. Perhaps she's mad already? I haven't been blamed. Nobody blames me. Nobody will. I haven't told a soul about the bee—my letting go of the ladder. She plays. I stay in my room and watch my mark. In the mark, I see a place in the past, before Mother died, before my brother was killed, before my sister hanged herself, before my girlfriend left me for another, before the dog took ill and had to be destroyed, before my aunt came to stay, before all that, I see in the mark, a dinner table with good food and enjoyable conversations that I have never thought to be grateful for. The last time we ate together—I think it was the last time—during our dessert, I spoke about my idea about how one could feed the blacks in the Sudan. I had watched a TV show on how to grow vegetables in the north. Northerners grew all kinds of things by mixing muskeg with sand. There are billions and billions of tons of muskeg up north. The Sudan has billions and billions of tons of sand. So, I told the family, all we have to do is ship muskeg over there and mix it up with the sand. Gardens will grow and nobody will starve. Father thought it was a great idea. He said I ought to write a letter to the Prime Minister. I did. Some thirty-six weeks later, I received a short reply from the Minister of Foreign Affairs, who thanked me for my suggestion, but reminded me that any such philanthropic ideas that might instigate the said increase of the South African population would be out of the question. That *this* government, like most governments, was concerned with lowering taxes—not with implementing plans that would enlarge the populations of poorer nations. In closing, he thanked me again for the letter, mentioning that he and his colleagues always enjoyed hearing from ordinary Canadians, and hoped that I would continue to remain a loyal ordinary Canadian and support their party. My mark. The colours are even brighter now. My aunt is still fingering the keyboard. I'll try to get out tomorrow. You can lose yourself in a room. You can lose yourself in anything coloured like a rainbow. What saves you? Maybe the view from the window: you look out and watch your neighbours cutting their lawns. No matter how much you've lost, or ache inside, they keep on cutting the grass. *Traditions. Generalizations.* Goodness me, what makes us fall in love with eyes? How mysteriously beautiful are people's eyes: blue and brown and green earths all by themselves. Yes, my mark on the wall. I know what it is now. My aunt put a crystal turtle on top of my bureau and the sun shines through.